Sherlo

a

Circus of Fear

# Sherlock Holmes
## and the
# Circus of Fear

## Val Andrews

**BREESE
BOOKS
LONDON**

First published in 1997 by
Breese Books Ltd
164 Kensington Park Road, London W11 2ER, England

© Breese Books Ltd, 1997

ISBN: 0 947533 17 6

Front cover photograph
is reproduced by kind permission of
Retrograph Archive, London

Typeset in 11½/14pt Caslon by
Ann Buchan (Typesetters), Middlesex
Printed and bound in Great Britain by
Itchen Printers Ltd, Southampton

# I

# Enter 'Lord' George

'Our caller, Watson, is, according to his visiting card, a peer of the realm.'

I was staying with my friend Mr Sherlock Holmes at the old rooms in Baker Street whilst my wife was visiting relatives. Moreover, I had placed my practice in the capable hands of a trusted locum that I might spend time with my old friend and perhaps even relive a little of the spirit of the halcyon days. We had breakfasted well, if in my case somewhat late, so that Holmes, although having long finished the first meal of the day, yet sat and gossiped as I still masticated. Our small talk was interrupted by a tread upon the stairs and the presentation by Billy of a visiting card.

I enquired, 'You doubt, then, the validity of the engraved words?' He passed the card to me for inspection and I observed that it was about four inches by five, and engraved upon buff stock. It bore the name Lord George Sanger and there was also an address in Finchley.

Holmes asked me, 'Did you ever encounter before a calling card of such formidable size, other than that of a tradesman?' I had to admit that it was indeed large for the card of a nobleman.

The page had no such doubts and he bowed and scraped our visitor into the room. Years of no game being afoot had made me ignore the message of the footsteps on the stairs, and I was expecting a tall, well-built man. No doubt Holmes was not surprised when our visitor turned out to be wiry and of less than average height. As he removed his silk hat I noted that it was custom made, very much higher than is usual and possibly so made in order to give an impression of a man taller than his five feet four inches. As Billy took it, along with the expensive-looking grey greatcoat, equally costly-seeming jacket and trousers were revealed. At his silk stock he sported a diamond-clustered pin and a gold watch-chain spanned his waistcoat.

'Lord George Sanger, I believe?'

Our caller answered Holmes in a voice that was gruff and far from aristocratic, yet with a ring of authority. 'Yes. Which of you is Sherlock Holmes?'

My friend said, 'I have that doubtful honour, sir, and this is my friend and colleague Dr John Watson.'

Sanger nodded to me curtly and occupied the chair which by gesture Holmes had indicated.

'Mr Holmes, I am going to be completely honest with you. I am not in fact a peer of the realm.'

Holmes nodded. 'I am aware of that, sir, for several reasons. The first that although your breeches were made in St James's, you hitched them at the knee on seating yourself.'

Sanger started. 'Why should I not, it is a common-sense action to avoid one's breeches from bagging at the knee.'

Holmes smiled as he said, 'Common sense, but not an action that one associates with the aristocracy. The same can be said for your evident habit of securing all of the buttons upon your waistcoat.'

Our visitor smiled, which caused the skin on his gaunt face to wrinkle, giving him an appearance not unlike that of an Eskimo or Red Indian. It was a face that had endured a lot of weather, much of it overwarm or extremely cold. It was a weather-beaten, seventy-year-old face as I now perceived, having thought him younger at a distance. What was left of his hair, and his neatly trimmed whiskers had been none too skilfully dyed and the application of this darkening agent had also been made to his eyebrows, the misapplication to one of them giving him a rather odd appearance which was completed by a rather obvious spot of rouge at each cheek. He said to Holmes, 'Well, sir, is there anything else that you can deduce from my appearance?'

Holmes smiled, more kindly, 'Not much, sir, save your long association with horses which the arrangement of callouses upon your palms tell me. Notice, Watson, that they are caused by many years of driving a team. Oh yes, and you have shown Her Majesty some service, indicated by the V.R. diamond pin at your stock. Although I'll wager you have never been listed in *Debrett's*, you call yourself a lord without fear of punishment, so evidently Her Majesty is aware of your use of the title and tolerates it. The Queen does not often bestow gifts upon commoners save in the case of soldiers, sailors and inventors. I do not believe that you fall into any of these categories. However, she has been known to have a fondness for showmen and I believe you fall into that mould. Your obvious association with horses makes me believe that you are possibly the owner of a travelling circus.'

Of course, looking back upon the incident I realize that most members of the public would have known of Sanger's

Circus at that time. However, Holmes and I moved in a world that was seldom brought into contact with such an enterprise as a travelling circus. It is my view that Sanger did not believe this to be possible and therefore underestimated some of Holmes's deductions. But he said nothing on such lines and got straight to the purpose of his visit.

'You are correct, Mr Holmes, however you came upon that fact. I am not only the owner of a circus but, dare I say, the most famous and impressive circus in the whole of Europe, if not the world. Over the past half-century I have built my enterprise from a one-man booth performance to a spectacle taking place in the largest tent ever made in the British Isles, with hundreds of magnificent horses, a score of camels, lamas, zebras, lions, tigers and several large elephants. Add to this a group of performers who are the best of their kind and you have Lord George Sanger's Circus. Naturally, although I am honest in my business dealings, my enterprise has long created envy, jealousy even, with the traditional circus families. You see, I was not born into the circus business, for my father operated a peepshow at the fairgrounds. Aye, and the fairground folk envy me too; yet none of these that I have mentioned would do me evil. Certainly they might over-paste my announcements or have me misdirected upon the road, but no, they would never wish me real harm . . .'

He paused, and after some seconds I dared to enquire, 'But you have enemies who might?'

He was again silent for some seconds, then he said, 'I would like to have been able to say no, Doctor, but in the light of recent events I cannot. It all started a few years ago when, in addition to my travelling circus, I was the owner of Astley's Theatre, just south of the River Thames. I operated the amphitheatre, with its circus and horse operas there for almost twenty years. Then I started to get threatening messages, sometimes written and sometimes by word of mouth. I ignored suggestions that I should quit Astley's, but in the end I was forced to do so. The authorities, doubtless through the persistence of informers, started what seemed like a campaign of persecution against me. Suddenly exit doors that had been perfectly sound for years were required to be replaced, gangways had to be enlarged and all my careful fire precautions deemed inadequate. Animal cages, perfectly practical for their purpose, had to be rebuilt or replaced, and stables, the envy of the equine world, were constantly criticized and all manner of changes demanded. I spent a fortune, Mr Holmes, on all these improvements and yet still in the end they were not satisfied. Suddenly there was this new authority, the London County Council; they wanted all my improvements altered and really made it financially impossible for me to carry on. So I sold the place for a very considerable sum. Since then Astley's historic amphitheatre has been demolished and I have reinvested the money in making my travelling circus even more magnificent.'

Holmes offered Sanger a cigar, from the coal scuttle, having observed the old-plated cutter which hung from the showman's watch-chain. He lit one himself also, and soon the room was filled with aromatic smoke. At least it was an improvement on the Scottish mixture.

Then Holmes said, 'Unfortunately, this campaign by your enemy or enemies (if such it was) appears to have succeeded all but a decade ago. It might be that I could have helped you back in 1892, but I fail to see how I can help you now.'

This time there was no lapse of time before Sanger replied, 'But, Mr Holmes, it has started all over again. Not content with ruining me at Astley's they are now determined to do the same thing to my travelling circus!'

Holmes, interested now, leant forward in his chair and asked, 'Is history repeating itself? I mean, are you getting threatening letters followed by visits from officious local authoritarians?'

The old showman shook his head, then after looking thoughtful said, 'Well, yes and no. Yes, I have received written and verbal warnings, but no, the misfortunes have been of a far more serious nature. For example, the guy ropes of my tents have been cut, animals deliberately released from their cages, and many of my performers have had accidents in the ring which have been engineered by a person or persons unknown.'

I butted in once more, despite Holmes's steely eye. 'Do you have any of the written threats to show us, Sanger?'

He said, 'Why, yes. I have the latest one which I received yesterday morning. It had evidently been posted under the door of my caravan during the night.' He took a piece of folded paper from inside his jacket. 'I have consigned all the previous messages to the fire, but I realize now that I should have kept them.'

Holmes took the paper from him and crossed to the table where he spread it carefully. He read aloud,

BETWEEN THE ENTRANCE OF THE SHEEP AND THE PLACE OF PROGRESS WILL THE NINTH LIFE BE WELCOME. PULL DOWN AND AVOID TROUBLE.

Holmes busied himself with his lens and then remarked, 'It is written, or rather printed, with indian ink upon stout paper of the kind used by artists. The words are written with a relief nib, associated more with writing than drawing, yet the ink and paper would have been suggestive of an artist. The paper was torn from a tablet by folding and scoring the paper between the nails of the finger and thumb. Despite being printed I think I can say that it has been written by a man rather than a woman. But let us for the moment try to decipher the meaning of the message.'

Sanger rose from his seat and made as if to leave, saying, 'Very well, sir, I will leave it with you, but I wonder if I might ask you to attend a performance of my circus tonight, for you will then have a better idea of what I am up against and what I have to try and protect. Come, we are at present playing at Romford, which is a small town in Essex. This is not a very long way off and I also feel that you would enjoy the experience.'

We exchanged glances and Holmes took my expression, quite correctly, to mean that I was agreeable. He nodded, 'Very well, my dear Sanger, I see no reason why we should not accept your invitation. You will, I assume, provide us with transportation?' Holmes was never afraid to demand those favours to which he felt entitled.

Sanger said, 'Of course. I will send my own carriage for you at about six. The performance is at eight, so you will thus have ample time to make the journey.'

After Sanger had departed my friend spread the threatening message before him upon the table. He said, 'Little point in taking any action, Watson, until we can discover what the message refers to. Sanger has no idea or he would not have brought it to me. The thing takes the form of an enigma or word puzzle rather than a code, I feel. The only part of it that springs at once to my mind is the mention of 'the ninth life'. According to legend, a cat has nine lives, so I assume that a feline of some kind is involved. You are more worldly than I in matters of public entertainment, Watson; would a circus feature sheep and cats?'

I shook my head, saying, 'I rather doubt it, Holmes. The last one I attended consisted mainly of feats performed by people and horses. There were clowns, jugglers, bareback riders, that sort of thing, and a performing elephant. But I suppose other circuses could have dancing sheep and acrobatic cats.'

Holmes ignored, or seemed to, my irony and returned to his study of the threatening message. 'Pull down and avoid trouble is of course obvious; Sanger is advised to fold up his tents and depart.'

Other problems and activities intervened so he was not much nearer to solving the puzzle by the time Sanger's carriage arrived to take us to the circus. We decided not to wear evening dress but none the less we took suitable trouble with our appearance; Holmes in a grey frock coat and I in a short black jacket and grey checked trousers. With suitable greatcoats we felt that we would show Sanger proper respect without appearing to be over-dressed. Yet once we had climbed into the carriage and noted its coat of arms upon the door and postilion sitting up at the rear we began to wonder is we should not have dressed for the opera!

When we reached Romford, passing vast open meadows on the way, I began to wonder if Sanger had picked the right place to hold his circus, but these doubts were dispelled by the sight of several hundred people lining up outside the entrance to the vast grey umbrella of a tent. We were shown to two ringside seats and I looked around me with interest, never having seen a circus which was on quite such a grand scale. There were, for instance, two main masts (which I would later learn to refer to as 'king poles') plus a couple of dozen lesser ones supporting this canvas shelter which seemed capable of seating at least a thousand people, mainly upon tiered wooden benches, plus seats like the ones that we occupied. As for the ring itself, this was about twelve yards across and enclosed by a circle of box-like sections no more than thirty inches high, topped with red velvet. Opposite to that gap in the canvas walling through which we had entered there was a red plush curtained entrance, rather like a small theatre, on top of which were half a dozen uniformed bandsmen, each with a brass instrument. They played well enough to satisfy the public on the benches yet badly enough to produce the odd wince from Sherlock Holmes when a particularly strident discord was produced.

Then, just as boredom was beginning to affect me, there was a shrill blast from a whistle and a top-hatted man in a pink hunting coat entered brandishing a long whip. He cracked the whip as he raised his silk headgear, and Sanger's Circus began!

I suppose it is true to say that having seen the performance so many times since, it is difficult to be subjective concerning my impressions of it on that first occasion. The circus is of course essentially an equestrian and equine affair and has been since Philip Astley started it all, back in the late eighteenth century. But whilst Astley was the 'father of the circus' George Sanger was one of the pioneers of its travelling version. In half a century Sanger had gradually taken his circus from being a fairground sideshow to its position as the circus in the British Isles. Only his brother, John Sanger, had an attraction on anything like the same scale. During John's lifetime the brothers had co-operated to make it possible for both of them to make a handsome living. Since John's demise in 1889 his descendants had proved less friendly, and a fierce rivalry between the two Sander circuses had sprung up.

However, all of this I would learn in the fullness of time and I must return to describing my impressions gained upon that night at Romford, so many years ago.

The ringmaster having cracked his whip there entered into the ring no less than eight cream-coloured ponies. These were directed by their trainer, who wore a French military uniform, to break them into smaller groups, twos and threes, and perform various gyrations and pirouettes. The ponies placed their forefeet upon the ring fence and circled it, repeating the manoeuvre with their hind hooves upon the fence. Finally, in turns they reared up onto their hind legs and slowly backed out. The act was striking, with the ponies in a minimum of harness (simply pale blue bridles, bearing reins and waistbands). The audience enjoyed this lively opening to the evening. Next came a satire of the number, with an extremely amusing clown in a spangled motley and pointed white hat, who presented a comedy horse of the kind which has two people inside it. This creature burlesqued everything which the ponies had done, including the backward hindleg walk which resulted in a calculated collapse of the two persons inside the horse skin.

After he had chased the horse out of the ring, the clown indulged in a whirlwind display of tumbling which quite took one's breath away, though seemingly not his. Then the band ceased playing for the first time since the circus had started and the ringmaster and the clown exchanged dialogue:

'I say, Mr Clown, you will have to go now. I want you to leave!'

'Then want must be your master!'

'Master? I *am* your master, master of the circus.'

'If you are my master, what am I?'

'What are you? Why you are a mere nobody.'

'Fine job you have got . . . master of nobody!'

'You are a fool.'

'Yes? Well, you are another!'

'What did you say?'

'I said, how's your brother, all right?'

'I must introduce the next act. Monsieur Duval, the famous contortionist, the world's greatest boneless wonder.'

'I know an even greater boneless wonder . . .'

'What is that?'

'A sausage!'

'Get out!'

The ringmaster cracked his whip and chased the clown from the ring as the band started to play a pleasant waltz and the contortionist bounded in, clad in a leotard and bringing with him a small pedestal which he placed in the centre of the ring. He leapt up onto this stand and bent over backwards to push his head between his legs to begin a most incredible series of contortions and impossible-seeming dislocations. Finally he stood on his hands, lowered himself on his elbows, picked up a top hat with his feet and placed it on his head.

Next a large spotted steed, looking for all the world like a rocking horse, came into the ring, followed by an attractive young woman in a ballet dress. The ringmaster assisted her onto the horse, which circled the ring whilst she stood upon its bare back. She took up many attractive balletic attitudes upon the moving horse, and then the clown ran in and started to interrupt.

'I say, Mister Ringmaster. That's a nice horse and a very charming young lady!'

'That is true, Bimbo, but what are you doing here?'

'I want to speak to the young lady.'

'Very well, but make it quick.'

'I've got a restitution, a resitution, a piece of poetry . . .'

The clown sank on one knee and, removing his dunce's headgear, addressed the equestrienne as she sat upon the back of the stationary horse.

> 'Oh you pretty little dear,
> Come and have some ginger beer!'

This angered the ringmaster who chased the clown from the ring. Then, after the rider had leapt through a series of paper-covered hoops, I turned to Holmes and said quietly, 'I wonder why the clown was brought in to such little effect?'

Holmes said, 'To give the lady a chance to regain her breath, Watson.'

The equestrian display was followed by a troupe of performing poodles, trimmed up in the French style with pompom tails, shaved middles and lion-like manes tied up with ribbon. A couple presented the dogs, which skipped, leapt and walked upon rolling spheres. I quite enjoyed their merry antics but I could see for the first time since the performance had begun, signs of displeasure in Holmes's facial expression. I knew of course that he was not over-fond of dogs, but I believe it was more the pointless nature of the performance which troubled him. But he bucked up when the flying trapeze act began. The performers not only flew from one trapeze to another, but also caught each other in mid-air in the style familiar to everyone. It was a dangerous performance, for the apparatus was stationed at least thirty feet above the grassy sawdust-sprinkled circle which formed the circus ring. As these aerial acrobats lowered themselves to the ring to take applause, the clown Bimbo appeared on the scene again, his strident voice raised, shouting, 'Let me have a go!'

Before he could be prevented he had shinned up a rope ladder and was swinging wildly from one trapeze in a most alarmingly dangerous manner. Another clown, in less splendid motley, in fact in a suit and facial make-up which made him look rather like a tramp, ran into the ring and climbed up to the trapeze opposite to where Bimbo swung. Whilst Bimbo hung to his trapeze by the backs of his knees he held his hands ready to catch his friend. The tramp swung several times to gain momentum, then flew across to be safely caught by Bimbo. The only mishap was that his voluminous trousers fell down, to reveal red, white and blue under-drawers. The audience gasped, then there was a shriek of laughter as the two merry men descended. The audience gave them the applause they deserved.

The first half of the programme (I consulted my hunter to discover to my amazement that we had been watching the circus for more than an hour) came to an end with a display of sedate poses and movements by two large Asian elephants. They sat up upon huge tubs, then stood on these first with their front feet and then with their back legs. Eastern music was played by the band and the elephants were suitably decorated with exotic finery. These trappings were removed from the pachyderms and a comic barbershop was set up, with huge brushes, razors and buckets of foam and water. The elephant trainer, Captain Swallow, announced that the elephants would be happy to shave any volunteer from the audience, but none was forthcoming. The tramp clown, evidently having retrieved his nether garment, walked into the ring, ruefully fingering his chin. The trainer seated him, draped a white cloth about his neck and one of the elephants removed his battered hat with the tip of its trunk. The other elephant applied foam, none too gently, to the tramp's face with a huge brush. The slightly smaller animal brandished the huge property razor but the tramp rose in protest. Seemingly without warning, the biggest elephant squirted water at his face from its trunk, into which it had evidently siphoned it during the lathering by its comrade!

An interval was announced, and we discussed what we had seen. Holmes remarked, 'It is a very big organization, Watson, and the performance is of an extremely high standard. But have you noticed how few human performers there are?'

I counted upon my fingers, 'The ringmaster, the principal clown, his foil, the contortionist, the horse trainer, the elephant trainer, the couple with the dogs, the two acrobats on the trapeze .... I make that ten performers, and the show is only halfway through.'

He shook his head. 'You forgot the lady rider, which would make your count eleven. But no, Watson, there have been less than that because the contortionist and the tramp clown are one and the same, the horse trainer is one of the canine couple, so the count is eight.'

Along with many of the rest of the audience we strolled through the ring entrance during the interval where we were invited to part with sixpence, which entitled us to inspect the stables and menagerie. This proved to be housed in an open-topped quadrant. There were horse lines which reminded me of my army days, though the beasts that I remembered were of a less exotic appearance, for here were piebald, skewbald, spotted and all-white horses. There were also mules and donkeys, not to mention the cream ponies that we had seen in the ring. There must have been a hundred horses at least, but when I wondered at this number Holmes said, 'I'll wager that two-thirds of them are for purposes of transportation.'

Of course, this big circus would require many cart-horses to haul it from one town to another. I wondered how many horses it would take to transport the elephants, but Sanger answered this question when he joined us before the two elephants which were rocking gently to and fro as they sifted hay with the tips of their trunks. They recognized Sanger at once and raised their trunks to him in salute. He patted their trunks and spoke gently to them. He shouted with rage at the elephant keeper because they had not enough water; his manner toward man and beast being quite different. He said, 'They walk from ten to twenty miles between tobers, according to the distance involved.'

I was quite surprised. 'Do they never run amok?'

He smiled, 'They are females, it is usually bull elephants that give trouble. Sometimes they stop and raid a cake stall or greengrocer's cart, but a few free passes usually patches things up. They walk slowly so they are always the first to leave one tober and the last to arrive at the next.'

Holmes enquired, 'How often does the circus move, Lord George?'

Then Sanger said that which made us both start. 'Every

day as a rule. With a circus of this size we can take in as many as are likely to attend in just two performances. Exceptionally we stay two days, or very rarely three.'

I was quite startled and showed my ignorance of such matters even further by asking, 'How many days do you allow for travelling and pulling down and re-erecting your tents and stuff?'

Sanger said, with the weariness of one with a lifetime of dealing with the public behind him, 'Dr Watson, we play six towns a week as a rule. For example, at the end of this performance we will pull down, load the wagons, grab a few hours' sleep, then at about 5 a.m. we will make the journey to Aldershot where we will build up and be ready for the first performance by afternoon.'

I was staggered, never having really thought too much about the comings and goings of a travelling circus.

Sanger proudly showed us his groups of lions and tigers, each animal in an individual section of larger travelling cages, partitioned from each other. But apart from these there was a larger cage on wheels, formed entirely of slim iron bars, without the wooden backing of the communal cages. This, we were told, was the portable performance cage which would be towed into the ring during the second half of the show.

'Wallace, the world's largest lion, will be put through his paces.' Sanger indicated the huge animal which paced within. 'He is a veteran, nearly twenty years old and soon to be retired.'

In my continued ignorance I assumed that the animal was pacing the cage from frustration at being imprisoned. But Sanger explained, 'He is pacing in anticipation, for his dinner is to be served at any moment.'

A man dressed in a warehouse coat arrived with a trolley upon which lay joints of meat. With a pitchfork he speared a larger joint than the others, which lay apart, and passed it through the bars into the cage. Wallace avidly grappled with the joint of meat and was soon demolishing it with some show of relish. Holmes observed, 'I see you feed your lions and tigers upon mutton, Lord George.'

The showman said, 'We take advantage of whatever good meat is available locally. At the moment in this area mutton is cheapest.'

After inspecting the camels and llamas we were escorted back to our seats to see the second half of the circus performance. This recommenced with a display of tumbling by a troupe of three acrobats, 'the Brothers Austin' (according to the ringmaster's announcement) who stood one upon the other's shoulders, jumping up to that position from ground level by means of a small springboard. As a finale they walked out of the ring, three men high! I turned to Holmes to get his reaction, but he was deep in thought and not really taking in the splendid display of acrobatics.

Suddenly he said, 'Watson, follow me, we may be in time to avert a tragedy!' He leapt from his seat and, ignoring protestations from performers and circus hands, he led me through the plush curtains and into the menagerie quadrant once again.

'Too late, Watson, I fear we are too late!' We stood before the lion's performance cage to see Wallace lying prone upon its floor and clearly no longer of this world. Performers in motley were crowded around the cage, but some of them were summoned away to the arena by the ringmaster. One of the three Austin brothers yelled, 'Quick, fetch Lord

George! I'm afraid poor old Wallace has breathed his last.'

Holmes inspected the clearly dead lion and turned to me. 'Watson, your observations would be appreciated. I know you are not a veterinarian, but I imagine you could hazard a guess.'

I looked carefully at the prone feline. 'Flecks of foam upon the mouth, dilation of the pupils. If he were a man I would diagnose poisoning. Probably cyanide, judging from the speed of its effect.'

Holmes nodded. 'My own feeling entirely.'

At this point I remembered that Holmes had brought me back to the menagerie before any sort of intimation of the event had occurred. I asked, 'What made you say that we might be in time to prevent a tragedy, Holmes?'

He replied, 'My dear Watson, I had been dwelling in my mind upon that ominous message that Sanger had received. Remember how it began, "Between the entrance of the sheep and the place of progress", I suddenly wondered if the entrance of the sheep could refer to the joints of mutton that we had been shown. "The place of progress" could be this performance wagon and I'm sure you have noticed that the circus folk refer to lions and tigers as "cats"? Well, "the ninth life" would indeed have been welcome. But evidently the tendency to have nine lives only applies to the domestic species. Elementary enough in retrospect, Watson, but I was too late in solving the riddle.'

Lord George appeared horrified at the sight of his splendid lion lifeless. He shouted, 'Austin, send for Bimbo, and you and your brothers must fill in when the lion act is due on the programme.'

Austin removed himself, doubtless to alert his brothers regarding their extra appearance on the programme. Bimbo the clown, still in his make-up and costume, arrived swiftly, and looked aghast at Wallace. The cage door was opened and he started to examine the dead lion.

Lord George explained, 'Everyone in my circus has more than one occupation. Bimbo is our vet, having been trained for that profession rather against his own wishes. He had always wanted to be a clown and had trained himself for that profession in secret. When he came of age he joined us, but we have found his ability to doctor the animals almost as valuable as his brilliance as a performer. If there is one member of my troupe that I could scarce do without, it is he!'

Bimbo came to the same conclusion as I had myself, anxiously inspecting the other big cats for signs of distress. He found none and said to Sanger, 'Whoever poisoned poor old Wallace evidently wished the other cats no harm.'

Holmes asked, 'Would the poisoner recognize the joint that was intended for Wallace by its very size?'

Bimbo said, 'Yes, and whoever did it would also know that Wallace's joints were always placed a foot or so apart. He always has the best meat there is, or rather did have.'

Holmes decided that we would forgo the pleasure of watching any more of the performance that we might concentrate upon that which we had learned. He told Sanger the sad fact that he had solved the riddle of the unsigned message just a shade too late. But Sanger, for such an impatient man, was remarkably forgiving, saying, 'Your solution was based upon facts that you only very recently learned.'

Of course we made a few routine enquiries of various members of the circus troupe and among the staff. Nobody had noticed any stranger to have been anywhere near the meat after its delivery by carter from the slaughterhouse just an hour before it was fed to the animals. Nobby Howes, the young man whose job it was to tend and feed the big cats, seemed above reproach, honest and open-faced with good said of him by all. He said, 'I can't see how the meat could have been poisoned when it was delivered, Mr Holmes, for the poisoned joint was clearly meant for old Wallace, wasn't it? In that case how would it be known at that stage which of the bigger joints he would get. There were several big 'uns, but I picked out the one with what I thought to be the best meat on it.'

Holmes asked, 'Who came near the meat after you had placed Wallace's portion aside from the rest?'

Howes scratched his head. 'Only Bimbo as far as I can remember, and a vet doesn't poison valuable animals, does he?'

But our enquiries were cut short by a sudden surge of activity around us. The second and final performance was over, the band was playing 'God Save the Queen' and even before the audience emerged from the big tent its side wallings were being dropped and the tober itself was a hive of activity. As the local people emerged, reluctantly, to return to their homes, everything was being packed and loaded into vehicles. Soon the tent was just a skeleton, and not even that for long as the two king poles were being lowered to the ground. Wooden shutters were being fastened to the barred fronts of animal cages by workmen who still had theatrical make-up on their faces. Within two hours Sanger's Circus, the biggest in the British Isles, or possibly in Europe, was just a circle of loaded wagons and caravans and a few score of graving horses.

During all this activity Sanger sat upon the top step of his caravan and shouted orders in his stentorian voice, as if through a megaphone . . . 'Nobby, board up those cats . . . Bimbo . . . keep that horse away from those flares . . . Charlie, get a move on with those canvas bales!' Yet he had time for us too, introducing us to his secretary, a Mr George Forrest. 'I'm not much for writing and so on, George does all that.'

We shook hands with the rather furtive, anxious-looking little man. His expression of anxiety I could understand, for I would hardly have relished being Sanger's secretary myself. The strange little man had those ink-stained fingers so typical of his kind. He left for his own caravan and we were left to speak with the meteoric circus owner.

Sanger took a folded paper from his pocket and handed it to my friend. 'There has been another unsigned note, Holmes, pushed under the door of my wagon during the performance.'

Sherlock Holmes spread the sheet of paper upon one of the lower caravan steps. I moved in close to him that I might read it . . .

STARS SHINE, STARS BRIGHT, WILL BE OUTSHONE TOMORROW NIGHT!

While we were pondering over this message Sanger was called away, excusing himself with a muttered, 'I will rejoin you within a few minutes.'

At least this gave me a chance to discuss the new puzzle with my friend. 'What do you make of it, Holmes?'

He pondered. 'We learned tonight, through the poisoning of that poor beast, that whoever we are dealing with means business. "Stars shine" could of course refer to stars of the circus ring, and "outshone" could point to the appearance of some rival attraction, meaning financial disaster for the circus in Aldershot. Yet I doubt it, fearing as I do some more sinister implication. What is brighter than a star, Watson?'

I was thoughtful, then said, 'Fire?'

He nodded and said, 'What could be more disastrous to a circus than fire?'

I was all for informing Sanger of Holmes's fear, but he forbade this, for reasons that I would not understand for quite a while.

When Sanger returned it was to tell us of an interview with a journalist from one of the more sensational newspapers who had managed so quickly to learn of the tragedy. 'I got as much use as I could from the incident, gentlemen. It was a tragic affair, but why not rescue some use from it?'

I sensed that Holmes disapproved, but he said little about the matter, instead informing Sanger, 'Whilst I myself have some essential work back in London, my colleague will return shortly to keep watch and take whatever action he sees fit.'

Sanger grunted, but said, grudgingly, 'Well, I suppose Dr Watson will help me as much as he can.'

Holmes bade me to fetch Lord George's carriage that we might return to Baker Street, where he would need to stop, but informed me that I would need to pack some necessities for a short tour with the circus. I agreed, though I own I was not exactly delighted at the prospect of sharing a tent and living out of a gladstone.

We discussed it all at length on the way back to London. I mildly remonstrated with Holmes concerning my part in the case. 'Holmes, I may have dreamed of running away with the circus as a child, but campaigning in Afghanistan and other places has cured me of any desire to live under canvas!'

Holmes chuckled. 'But you will not be under canvas, Watson, at least not at night, for you will sleep in a splendid caravan which you will share with Bimbo the clown. I want you to observe everything that goes on about you and to act upon your own good sense. You may of course send for me if you deem it essential.'

# II

# The Circus of Fear

By the time I had rejoined Sanger's Circus on the following day at Aldershot it was well after noon, and I had insisted upon taking the train rather than again go through the ritual of being fetched to travel in Sander's carriage. I was shown to Bimbo's caravan and told by a tent hand that I was to make myself at home until the clown returned.

I had soon unpacked and discovered a note pinned to one of a pair of bunk beds. 'This one is yours, Doctor, and so is the red cupboard'.

One of a pair of cupboards was painted red, the other blue, so I had no problem in finding where to hang my coats and breeches. My stockings and linen I left in my carpet bag, my spare boots I placed at the bottom of the red cupboard. Then I emerged to take a look around. Whilst the big tent was erected, along with the menagerie quadrant, I sensed that there were very few of the circus staff about, and none of the performers. When I asked the tent hand who had shown me where to unpack where everyone had gone he looked at me in bewildered amazement, 'Why, to parade of course!'

Soon I was to learn what he meant when the parade returned to the tober. There were wagons which rivalled those floats beloved of the organizers of carnivals in Venice and Monte Carlo. The first to return had a living lion with a lady dressed as Britannia sitting beside. The vehicle was splendidly decorated with gold leaf on mouldings, as were most of the vehicles which followed it. Each of these was drawn by a team of splendid horses, some by pairs but most by four in hand. There were cages of animals, floral floats and many splendid carriages. Between each vehicle walked either an exotic animal or a clown with a comic vehicle of some kind. There appeared to be far more to this free spectacle than was to be seen in the circus itself. Finally, Lord George followed in his other carriage, which was gilded rather like the coronation vehicle of state. Which reminds me that I am wrong to say finally because last of all there was a glass coach containing splendid crown jewels, or, I assumed, replicas of them.

Sanger greeted me brusquely, enquiring if my quarters were satisfactory. He said, 'You'll have to find your own way about, for I have my own problems. A new member of the troupe arrives today. The band has been a bit ragged this season. We've never had a conductor, but I feel that we need one to keep them a little more together!'

I made the mistake of agreeing that the band could be improved. He grunted. 'Humph, well, do whatever you want to, I must get on with my work!'

I decided that I would attend the first performance, if only to see what I had missed the night before; yet also wishing to keep an eye open. I must tell the reader that the second half of the performance was even better than the first, featuring as it did what Sanger later referred to as a hippodrama. This took the form of a playlet, 'Dick Turpin's Ride to York'. All the company took part, with the horse trainer as Dick Turpin and

Bimbo as his comic friend. Turpin rode furiously round the ring on a beautiful black horse, managing ultimately to bring all number of circus tricks into his performance. His saddle was stolen so he had to ride from London to York barebacked, and as he had not the price of the toll, he had to make the horse leap over the toll gate! There was a real coach for him to hold up, and of course he eluded the hangman for a happy ending.

It was so enthralling that it was not until the circus finale, with so many horses and ponies circling the ring, that I noticed the conductor, mentioned by Sanger, had not only arrived but had lost no time in getting to work. He was tall and spare of figure with a fierce black moustache. He wielded his baton with a lively style and I can honestly say that the band seemed a great deal more proficient under his control.

Bimbo made us a meal, as he called it, of toasted cheese and slices from a cottage loaf. He was a bright, intelligent fellow, and we got on quite well. Then it was on with the motley for him again, for the second of the day's performances. As Bimbo whitened his face with zinc oxide and blackened his brows with the soot from beneath the kettle, I wandered the tober seeking inspiration and information.

Through most of the second performance I kept up this activity, but tiring and having seen nothing to make me suspicious I decided to take a last look inside. The Dick Turpin spectacle was about midway through and I sat upon a space on one of the rear benches just to think things over. Suddenly I was roused from my reverie by a completely unexpected change in tempo from the band. In place of the Merry England piece, befitting the Turpin horse opera, they suddenly broke into an ear-piercing military march. I thought my eardrums would burst.

Another surprise was in store, for quite suddenly there was a torrent of water forcing itself against the wallings of the tent, rather as if a freak storm had occurred. The audience became truly alarmed.

Dick Turpin leapt from Black Bess's back and shouted, 'Don't panic, ladies and gentlemen. It's all part of the show!' But of course it was not.

I emerged from the tent to find the strange sight of charred tent wallings, yet the canvas was soaking wet. I looked around me to see numerous urchins with water buckets, stirrup pumps and all manner of water containers large and small.

So there had been both fire and water, within less than a minute of each other. Someone had fired the tent, and someone else had organized a veritable army of juvenile fire-fighters. Taking this in I looked around for other suspicious sights and sounds. I saw the retreating figure of Bimbo the clown going out of sight behind some wagons. I called, 'Bimbo, Bimbo!'

To my amazement he was soon by my side, and was in another costume, the one he wore as the comic character in the Turpin sketch. I said, 'Upon my word, Bimbo, I thought for a moment that you were a fire-raiser.'

He gasped, 'Not I, Doctor, but I don't quite understand the events of the past few minutes.'

I told him of the retreating figure in his spangled motley and he said, 'Someone must have wanted you to think I was the ohmy who started the fire. I must go to the wagon and see if my costume is there.'

We both went, and sure enough Bimbo's splendid spangled clown dress was hanging, exactly where he told me he had left it. He said, 'Some rascal must have borrowed it, just for a few minutes.'

I replied, 'Not this one, for he ran through mud and puddles which would make the costume dirty. We are looking for another costume, exactly like it.'

Bimbo said, quite simply, 'I have only the one, and Lord George himself presented it to me saying there was not another like it anywhere.'

And so it transpired that the circus had not only its enemies but its guardian urchins, who had disappeared as swiftly as they had come upon the scene. I discussed the episode with Sanger, but he was impatient to get to his wagon where he said he was about to hold a conference for journalists to give information regarding the fire.

That night I sank down upon my bunk, but found sleep difficult; a thousand thoughts seemed to plague my mind. Where had the boy fire-fighters come from, where had they gone, who had started the fire and how, why did someone want Bimbo to take the blame for it all, and why had the band suddenly struck up a different tempo? Above all else should I contact Sherlock Holmes; for quite a lot had happened since I had seen him. Sleep came at last, to be all too quickly shattered by Bimbo crashing about, making ready for the morning's journey to Camberley.

Once we reached the thriving little town I wondered if it was big enough to draw sufficient people for Sanger's enterprise. But the showman told me, 'We always do well here. There are several villages nearby from which the people come too; Yateley and Crowthorne to name but two, and there are farms around from which the farmers tend to bring all their workers for a treat.'

But after the parade Sanger hurried over to me and brandished yet another coded threat, written in the same style as the two I had seen before.

THE FALL OF THE WINGED. NOT SO EASY. GET OFF THE ROAD!

I wired Holmes at Baker Street to the effect that there had been a fire which was averted, and that I believed I could decode the new threat.

He replied: 'VERY BUSY STOP DO WHAT YOU CAN STOP REGARDS HOLMES'.

I felt that 'the winged' could refer to the word 'fly', and 'easy' led me to think of the flying trapeze. This was suggested to me by the words of the music hall ballad 'The Daring Young Man on the Flying Trapeze'.

My next step was considered carefully, especially when I peeped into the tent to see Bimbo, still in costume from the parade, climbing down from the trapeze rig. When I waved to him he disappeared through the curtains of the artists' entrance and I was unable to catch up with him. However, I saw him a few minutes later back at the caravan which we shared, where he was changing from his clown suit prior to removing his make-up. I confronted him by saying, 'Why did you avoid me back in the tent when I saw you climbing down from the trapeze rigging?'

He looked at me quite blankly, which, considering his white oxide, was not difficult for him. 'Dr Watson, I have just returned from the parade and have been nowhere near the tent. Ask anyone around here. I have scarcely been out of sight.'

I decided to take a chance and confide in Bimbo concerning the threatening note and my fears regarding the trapeze rig. As he splashed his face from a water bowl and wiped away the blanching agent with a towel, he said, 'If we warn anyone and the apparatus is checked the incident will not take place tonight and you will not stand a chance of catching any culprit. In fact you will possibly just defer the incident to a time when there is no expectation. But I know a way in which you can leave things to happen, but without risk.' He was a bright intellect and I was glad that I had confided in him, when he said, 'The aerialists can be safely warned and sworn to secrecy; for they would hardly be responsible for risking death by such means. The thing to do is to ensure that a net is rigged, for this performance only. It is always their boast that they perform without a net, but I feel sure they would agree.'

I pondered. 'Might it not be better to say nothing to them and rig the net to ensure their safety, doing it of course at the very last minute?'

He shook his head. 'If a trapezist falls into a net without doing it in the right manner he can be almost as badly injured as if he hit the ground. But if he is expecting to fall he will do it in the right way.'

The thought was a good one and I decided to use it. But how was I to set about it without alerting possible wrong-doers? I asked Bimbo if there was such a thing as a trapezist's net on the tober. He said that there was and that it had been used for another trapeze act the previous season. 'It's in the green pantechnicon, near the entrance gate.'

Yet knowing that it was there and working out a way to bring it into use without arousing general knowledge of its existence was another thing. But in the end, Bimbo and I worked out a plan.

The clown explained to me how the net was rigged. 'It is supported by four short poles, one at each corner, and the whole thing is pulled taut and supported by guy ropes. Its erection is the work of thirty seconds in the right hands. We could stow it under the tiered seating and produce it at the right time. I know four tent hands that I feel sure we can trust who might be entrusted with this task. All you have to do is give them the signal.'

Of course I felt bound to tell Sanger of our plans and Lord George, dubious at first, warmed gradually to the whole idea. He said, 'Leave it to me, Watson. I will stage it well so that nobody, save a handful of trusted workers, knows anything.'

That night, just as the poodles were making their mad scamper from the ring and back to their quarters the ringmaster began his introduction to the trapeze act. Then, when he got to the words, 'Without a net!' he was interrupted by the appearance near the ringfence of a fully-clad man, miserable of expression, who insisted, 'Stop, this act cannot go on without a net. Men, fetch the net!' The lugubrious band conductor, with great presence of mind tapped his baton and started the band playing 'Ta Ra Ra BoomDeAy' at a spanking tempo. The net was erected as Bimbo had predicted in little more than half a minute. Lord George came out, complete with silk hat and cane, gesticulating and arguing with the interrupters. But soon he shrugged and signed to the ringmaster to carry on. That worthy repeated his announcement, of course leaving out that which referred to the absence of a net.

The acrobats shinned up to their perches and went through the simple part of their display. They appeared to have been as surprised as anyone by the recent events but managed to calm themselves well. Then, as the horse-trainer-cum-trapeze artist flew from one trapeze to the bar of the second, one gave way under the pressure that his hands put upon it. Of course I knew that he was not taken completely by surprise, but the audience gasped, many rising to their feet at the horror of the falling acrobat. But as he landed neatly in the net, rolling over as he did so, there were more gasps, but this time they were those of relief.

After the performance there was a crowd of newspaper reporters all but fighting to speak with Lord George who dealt with the whole episode with incredible ease and poise. 'I have been imploring the Flying Vanbards to use a net for weeks. Well, tonight the local authorities took the matter, providentially as it transpires, out of my hands. A tragedy was averted, but Vanbard assures me that the tampering with his apparatus which was responsible for the incident will not occur again, as he will personally inspect it before each performance. So there will still be no net used, except where local authorities insist.'

One of the reporters, an aggressive-looking man, said, 'Lord George, what have you to say to the fact that I have enquired at the town hall and police station and can say that the local authorities were not involved. There is no local ruling about dangerous trapeze acts!'

Sanger brushed him aside. 'I have much to do making ready for the second performance, gentlemen, so you will excuse me now . . . believe me.' There was a steely glint in his eye which did its intended work.

Sanger invited me to his wagon where he served me with tea from a silver pot, in a porcelain cup with rampant lions painted upon it. 'Dr Watson, I have to congratulate you upon a brilliant deduction worthy of your friend Sherlock Holmes, which has saved me from presiding over a tragic accident, a fatality even, instead of a press coverage which will be of extreme value.'

His words were interrupted by a knock upon the caravan door which Sanger opened to reveal the tall figure of the new band conductor barely framed in it. 'Ah, Mr Conductor, pray enter. What can I do for you?'

The lanky maestro winked at me and said, 'It's more of a case of what I can do for you really, Lord George.' He spoke in a husky voice. 'You know, since I have been with your circus I have observed a great deal, both from that high bandstand perch, from the parade band wagon and just from being about the tober.'

Sanger looked at him keenly and motioned to him to be seated. The fellow sat down and removed his bandsman's cap. Lord George said, 'Well, you have done your job well; I always knew that we needed a conductor and the band has sounded greatly improved under your baton. Also you are quick-witted, covering recent breaks in the performance with hastily improvised playing. Oh, don't think I don't notice these things.'

The fellow had a crafty expression on his bony face and he smiled a rare, for him, smile which gave his drooping moustache a strange appearance. He said, 'I saw the signs that you intended to fire your own tent with the spirit from the flare lamps. It was I who recruited the urchins to act when given the sign.'

Sanger's eyes were wide, 'Sign? What sign, sir?'

The conductor replied, 'I knew that I would spot the very first flicker of flame from the bandstand, so I arranged to suddenly break into that military march as a signal for the water to be brought into play.'

Sanger was bristling with anger now. 'Why would I set fire to my own circus?'

The bandsman said, 'You did not intend complete destruction, just enough to make headlines in all the papers. The urchins took the cream off the top as it was. Just as the edge was taken from the publicity which an injured or dead acrobat would have yielded. Dr Watson, I understand, saw Bimbo the clown climbing the rigging earlier today.'

Sanger exploded, 'Oh, so not content with making ridiculous accusations against me you are now accusing the finest clown in Britain of unlawful deeds.'

The fellow shook his head. 'It was not Bimbo, as Watson has convinced himself, but someone of similar height and build wearing his make-up and costume.'

I felt compelled to speak at this point. 'Look here, Bimbo was wearing his costume at the time!'

He said, 'Just as he was wearing it when you proved that he would have it streaked with mud! The costume you saw is this one, still spattered a little, but cleaned up a bit.'

The bandleader pulled open a cupboard to reveal the still slightly spattered clown costume, identical otherwise to that worn by Bimbo.

Sanger was in a fine range now, 'Just what are you suggesting?'

The bandmaster said, 'That you yourself impersonated Bimbo, wearing this duplicate costume on several occasions.'

Sanger sneered. 'I am in my seventies . . . I may be of diminutive height like Bimbo, but I could scarcely climb the rigging or run through the tober at breakneck speed, and would I poison my own lion?'

Much the same points had been passing through my own mind and I said, 'Think, sir, think before you speak further and involve yourself in serious trouble through your accusations.'

He said, 'Doctor, Lord George has been an acrobat in his time, and despite a gammy leg and three score years and ten he is still quite capable of these things that he has denied. The threat notes were even self-produced and delivered.'

Lord George breathed hard. He was calmer now. 'Sir, I would not care to admit this unless it was necessary for me to clear your mind of such absurd thoughts, but, well . . . I am scarce able to read or write: my active life never allowed time for formal education. Why, I have to employ a secretary to handle the simplest of clerical duties.'

But his tormentor had an answer for this too. 'A secretary who was so deeply in your confidence as to write these notes for you. He wrote them in indian ink, which he uses extensively, as may be seen from the stains upon his fingers.'

I had to agree that this was so, having observed the clerk's fingers myself. There was just one doubt left in my mind; that of the poisoned lion. It is true that Holmes and I had known that Bimbo had been seen near the meat trolley, but I failed to see how this lanky music master could know, having not been upon the scene at that early stage in the investigations.

I expressed this feeling and added, 'I will now need to contact my friend Sherlock Holmes, the famous Baker Street detective, who will have many questions for you, sir!'

Suddenly a familiar voice rang through the wagon, 'None that I cannot answer, my dear Watson!' As he spoke the bandmaster started to peel a false nose fashioned from thin rubber and a false moustache. He followed this by removing two beetling eyebrows, to reveal the familiar features of Sherlock Holmes; familiar enough anyway, despite certain cosmetic elements to his normal complexion!

'Holmes, how could you?' I could scarcely say more in my astonishment. I remembered another occasion, some years before on the moors when Holmes had pulled a similar trick upon me. But in casting my mind back I remembered that he had been correct in his assurances that my presence upon those inhospitable moors near Baskerville Hall had been invaluable to him. Comparison showed me that the same was true concerning the circus episode. So instead of remonstrating I merely asked, 'Who answered the wire?'

Holmes chuckled and said, 'Mycroft had instructions to send you an answer more or less to that effect whatever your message: I trust you both implicitly, Watson; with two such stalwarts I could not have gone far wrong.'

When I had recovered a little from my astonishment I ventured to say, 'All becomes fairly clear to me now, save how you managed to raise that army of fire-fighters in such a short time.'

Holmes answered, 'The irregulars, Watson. I was expecting a fire, so I brought them down on the milk train.'

I shrugged and added, 'But how about the lion? I realize that Lord George must have poisoned it himself, but would any amount of publicity be worth the price paid in the loss of such a magnificent creature?'

Lord George was gradually recovering his composure and it was he who answered the question. 'Dr Watson, the animal was old and almost blind. To destroy it was really a kindness; that is why I chose Wallace to be one of the series of tragedies. I have done similar things before. When I owned Astley's Theatre I had an aged horse put down and released several wolves to make it seem that they had killed it. The publicity made for full houses with audiences wanting to see "The wolves that terrified London"! Business in the circus may look brisk to you, and it is indeed quite fair, but I need it to be more than that. Yes, Holmes, I admit that I have done everything that you have accused me of, and would do the same again, for business has started to get brisker, and these news stories will continue in their value throughout the season. A showman, a real showman such as myself, thrives upon notoriety and bluff. Yet I would not want the public to know that I had organized these near-tragedies myself. What must I do to obtain your promise not to reveal the fact?'

Holmes breathed hard and deep. 'Lord George, I cannot help but wonder at how you would have dealt with your conscience had the aerialist been killed, and women and children been burned to death had the small planned fire burned out of control. You have a completely ruthless streak in you, sir. But I am willing to remain silent if you are agreeable to certain suggestions of mine.'

It was as if the detective had thrown the ruthless showman a lifeline. He grasped at this extended straw. 'I am a wealthy man, Mr Holmes, yet I cannot offer you financial reward in return for your silence, for I know that you would not accept it. Indeed, I have already placed your fee in this bag; for I am astute enough to know what it is and that you never vary it save where you decide to omit it entirely.'

He placed the bag upon the shelf which dropped from the wall to serve as a table. 'Now, sir, I am in your hands, a man of straw. Please tell me your conditions.'

Sherlock Holmes considered carefully before he replied, then he said, 'Lord George, I want your word that you will never again endanger life in the quest for notoriety, publicity or public acclaim. I shall keep an eye on the newspaper headlines and I will soon know if your word is not your bond. Should this appear to be so I shall make known your recent actions. You know, Sanger, Barnum may have said that it matters not what is said about you so long as it is said, but I am eloquent enough to knock that theory into a cocked hat should I be required to do so.'

Sanger nodded and said, 'I agree to your condition unreservedly. I will even sign a paper to that effect should you require it.'

Holmes replied, 'That will not be necessary, Lord George. But come, you have heard only one of my conditions.'

The circus king raised an expressive eyebrow and said, 'I am but putty in your hands, sir, so name them.'

There was a wicked twinkle in Holmes's eye as he said, 'I have a group of street arabs whom I refer to collectively as the Baker Street irregulars. They were responsible for extinguishing your fire and on many occasions I have been glad of their services. They are rough diamonds, my dear Sanger, as Watson will agree.' I nodded. 'Yet they can be depended upon in an emergency.'

I nodded again. Holmes continued, 'Well, far too many of them wish to become detectives or investigators in general. Since they saw your street parade some of them have expressed a desire to become circus artists or workers of some kind. There is little future for most of them in the big city. It would be a real kindness if you could adopt a few of them. I do not mean that you should take them into your family, but just into your circus, as apprentice boys and girls, so to speak. I feel sure that they would train up into first-class riders, acrobats, or even just humble tent hands. It would be so much better for them than roaming the streets and turning ultimately to crime.'

Sanger was taken by surprise and so was I. Of course I knew that there was wisdom and humanity in Holmes's request. It was true that some of our unofficial detectives would some day go for soldiers or become policemen. But far too many would be left to a miserable adult life of crime. Sanger was surprisingly sanguine about it all. 'If they can rough it and sleep under the wagons, I'll take ten of them into my fold!'

To my astonishment Holmes insisted on conducting the band for the second performance of Sanger's circus that night, complete with his false nose and imitation moustache, and was to repeat the performance about a week later when we took a private horse omnibus full of irregulars down to the little town of Newbury where the circus was playing by then. The urchins sat, stood, jumped and generally misbehaved themselves upon several rows of plank seating. Some of the items in the performance bored them a little, being used to a fast-paced London gutter existence. But they laughed immoderately at the antics of Bimbo, and gasped in admiration at the exploits of the trapezists. They made great fun of Sherlock Holmes, knowing the lanky bandleader to be he!

From their reactions George Sanger picked out the ten that he thought might best take to circus life and the rest of us returned to London without them. They had no luggage, for their possessions were so few, but Sanger had promised to clothe and otherwise see to their well-being.

Back at Baker Street we mused upon the events of the past two weeks and Holmes said, 'I hope that we don't get too much involved with Lord George Sanger in the near future. I did not take too well to circus life, especially that caravan that I shared with the horse trainer.'

I said, 'Surely luxurious accommodation compared with your sojourn in the Stone Age hut on Dartmoor.'

My friend winced. 'I had hoped you might not bring up the subject of my surprise reappearances: I owe you a big apology, Watson, but you must admit that you learned a great deal. In fact, when I retire from this peculiar occupation of mine you might do worse than take over from me.

This talk of retirement forced me to say, 'Come, Holmes, we are much of an age you and I.'

He retorted, 'Quite so, but I have a feeling that you are built of sterner stuff than I. I can picture you wishing to continue in some of profession into quite old age.' Then he became more serious. 'I do intend to retire whilst still little more than middle-aged, Watson; I plan to leave the scene with my mental abilities and faculties at their height.'

I pooh-poohed what he was saying. 'What on earth would you do? Why, you always go to pieces when there is no crime to investigate!'

He was earnest, though. 'Watson, I shall keep bees and meditate, and write at least a dozen monographs. I already have my eye upon a farm cottage with an acre or two in Sussex, not far from Eastbourne, yet far enough for that distance to insulate me from the hordes of mankind.'

Revealing and unexpected as the turn that his words had taken might be, we were yet unable to dismiss from our minds and converse the circus adventure that had so roused us and summoned up our blood. Upon that subject, I said, 'By the way, Holmes, you have the advantage of me in having actually participated in a number of circus performances, even if in a musical rather than acrobatic capacity.'

He smiled and said, 'Not only that, Watson, but of course as musical director I actually took part in a number of those magnificent street parades for which Sanger is justly famous. What a splendid spectacle; who that has witnessed it could ever forget the splendid band wagon, the float bearing Britannia and the lion, or of course that magnificent crystal coach with its display of facsimile crown jewels. Do you know, Watson, I discovered, quite by accident, that the glass doors of that vehicle had no locks. Anyone determined enough could have stolen those splendid replicas!'

The reader might be tempted at this point to believe, as indeed we did ourselves, that our involvement with George Sanger was at an end. In some ways I wish it were so. Yet in the fullness of time we were to become once more concerned regarding the meteoric little showman.

# III

# Tragedy at Finchley

Curiously, Sherlock Holmes and George Sanger both retired within months of each other. The showman had always said that he would go out on a high note; the detective that he would cease work at the very height of his intellectual powers. Sander had his best-ever tenting season in 1904 and decided to retreat to his winter quarters at Finchley with the applause and acclaim of public and press still ringing in his ears and weighed down with takings. Having no male heir to carry on the tradition he decided to hold a sale of his animals and circus equipment at which he gained excellent prices. Retaining the control of his zoo at Margate and his theatres there and at East Ham he settled to the life of a farmer, soon creating alarm and dismay among his agricultural workers. They soon became somewhat surly when expected to put in the hours and energy usually displayed by circus staff! But all this we would only learn in the fullness of time.

As for Sherlock Holmes, well he had already set up his own retirement plan, leaving the bustle of Baker Street for the contrasting tranquillity of Fowlhaven, near Eastbourne in Sussex, in order to meditate and keep bees. But although both men had decided to rest following very full and eventful careers there was great variance in their ages: Sanger was eighty, whilst Holmes had barely reached his half century. The circus owner had bowed to practicality and good sense, whilst the detective had left his scene with good grace.

I heard nothing more of Sanger until the late autumn of 1911. At the time I was spending a few days with my friend Sherlock Holmes at his delightful cottage at Fowlhaven. We were taking a late breakfast when I remarked upon the fact that the morning papers had not yet arrived. Holmes said, 'Come, Watson, my dear fellow, make allowance for this sleepy community; you are not in London now. So much can occur to delay their delivery, such as Hargraves's cattle escaping from their field and blocking the road, or the duckpond flooding and creating all manner of problems. But I hear the sound of the garden gate being opened and the footsteps of Billy the paper boy. It is a pity that he had to walk most of the way and wheel his bicycle along my hand. A puncture no doubt, and he had forgotten to bring his repair outfit.'

I hastened to the cottage door and opened it to spare the papers the damage usually resultant from being pushed through the flap. Billy stood there, sheepishly, saying as he handed me the papers, 'Sorry I'm late, guv'nor! Tell Mr Holmes that I got a puncture and found that I had forgot to check that I had my repair stuff . . . and I 'adn't. I had to push the bike all up the hill.'

As I handed the papers to Holmes he saved my enquiry by saying, 'Come, Watson, the boy's boots make a noise like a horse upon cobbles as a rule. Obviously today their sound was muffled by a thick coating of mud. The rest was obvious. Had his lateness been due to the cattle or a flood this would not have resulted in the tundra-style quantity of mud required to muffle his hob nails. A puncture was the obvious answer, and he is a very forgetful lad. Makes his namesake at Baker Street seem like young Bertrand Russell!'

Holmes, even in retirement, had catholic tastes in newspapers; there were three of them, *The Times*, the *Daily Telegraph* and the *Daily Mirror*. I took up the latter, leaving the heavyweights to my friend. Ignoring the sensational headline of the day, my eye was quickly attracted to a piece concerning our old friend Lord George. I started, and exclaimed aloud, 'By Jove, Holmes. Poor old Sanger has departed this world!'

At my words Sherlock Holmes lowered his copy of *The Times* and replied, 'Oh dear. How sad, Watson. But he must have been a great age; perhaps four or five and eighty?'

I nodded, 'Yes, but evidently he was murdered rather than passing peacefully away!'

I read the piece aloud to Holmes, it being a short one . . .

### DAY-LONG HUNT FOR SHOWMAN'S SLAYER

#### Police Search Woods and Drag Ponds for Man Who Attacked Lord George Sanger and Two Employees

From Euston Road to the borders of Hertfordshire, the police were engaged all day yesterday in a man-hunt. They were searching for the man who, on Tuesday night, killed Lord George Sanger, the famous showman, at his home, Park Farm, Finchley, and badly injured two of his employees named Jackson and Austin.

The following description of the wanted man — an employee on the farm — was issued yesterday by the police: Wanted for murder, 28th, Herbert Cooper, 6 ft, twenty-six: complexion, hair and medium moustache dark; smart military appearance, may be taken for an actor or city clerk; recently worked as a labourer; dressed dark blue suit, light cap; clothing probably blood stained; had money and may endeavour to leave the country.

Lord George Sanger was sitting in his parlour, and one of his men, named Jackson, was reading to him. Suddenly Cooper ran in, armed with an axe. First he attacked Jackson with the axe, seriously injuring him. Then he attacked Lord George Sanger and inflicted several wounds, which caused the aged showman's death.

Jackson meanwhile rushed out. Cooper pursued him and tried to cut his throat with an open razor, the blade of which had been fixed with a piece of wood, inflicting several wounds.

Then Austin — one of the Austin brothers well known in the circus ring as bareback riders — came out to the porch of the house. Cooper at once attacked and injured him severely with the axe, after the razor was broken. Then Cooper made off.

Jackson, severely wounded as he was, managed to get to the street and summon aid. Doctors and police came. They found Mr Sanger insensible, by the gate, to which he had crawled, terribly wounded, and Austin, also insensible.

After treatment, Lord George Sanger recovered sufficiently to enable his dying depositions to be taken, but from the first there was no hope.

Austin and Jackson were treated at the farm, and the former was subsequently removed to the Great Northern Hospital. Subsequently he recovered sufficiently to be removed to a friend's house. Both men were making good progress last night.

It is suggested that Cooper may have been jealous of Jackson, who had recently replaced him as personal attendant and confidential friend of his master. Cooper previously had valeted Lord George Sanger and attended him to market and to the city.

All yesterday Cooper's father and brother were working at the farm as usual.

## Search Night and Day

Every available man in the S. Division, which extends from Euston Road to the borders of Hertfordshire, with its head-quarters at Albany Street, was searching yesterday for Herbert Cooper, the man wanted for the murder of Lord George Sanger.

Chief Inspector Kane of Scotland Yard visited the scene in the afternoon and made a close examination of the parlour in which Lord George Sanger was attacked. It was drenched with blood.

The search was prosecuted throughout the night of the murder by bodies of searchers carrying lanterns to assist them. They returned at dawn yesterday, exhausted by their labours.

They carried pitchforks to assist them in probing the under-growth. The search was being continued yesterday over a wider area, as Cooper was a very powerful, vigorous man, and may have walked a considerable distance.

There are many ponds and a stream which have been dragged, and there are two woods of considerable size which have been thoroughly searched. At early hours yesterday morning two gentlemen in tall hats were searching these woods narrowly. A possible clue was afforded by a circumstantial story of a green-grocer, with whom the wanted man had had business transac-tions. This man stated yesterday that he was driving up Highgate Hill on Tuesday night, shortly before seven o'clock, when he met Cooper riding a bicycle in the direction of London. Both the greengrocer and the boy who was with him are positive that the man was Cooper.

Mr James Crockett, a well-known showman and circus proprietor, who is a nephew of the dead showman and son of Lord George Sanger's sister, told the *Daily Mirror* yesterday that the old gentleman had been in good health, except that two or three weeks ago he had some internal congestion, from which he had, he believed, recovered. He saw him last on Tuesday week. He knew Cooper and his father quite well, and, like all the other relatives, was completely mystified by the crime.

Nobody saw Cooper go and Jackson is unable to say in which direction he went. Consequently there is nothing whatever to guide the search. Cooper is believed to be armed with a revolver. He left both the axe and broken razor behind him and also a revolver but is believed to have another one on him. It is believed that he had money and there is nothing to prevent him having gone away by train, for there was no general hue and cry for several hours after his disappearance. Cooper was charged some little time ago with violently assaulting a student and two friends who were crossing one of Sanger's fields, and setting dogs on them. He was charged but Sanger said in evidence that he was a good workman and he was only fined instead of being sent to prison.

### Tore Up Photograph

Cooper was a betting man and had lost a good deal of money lately over it. There is a rumour that he was inquiring last week about booking a passage to Australia. He was very discontented with his position, and he was very vain and fond of showing off in all sorts of ways. He used to stand on the seat of a bicycle and walk on his hands and do things of that kind. A girl with whom he was acquainted was so disgusted yesterday morning on hearing of the crime that she seized his photograph and tore it up.

There seems to be an idea that Cooper may have made for Liverpool Street or Charing Cross to get the Continental trains, but the police are absolutely at a loss. He may have gone into the provinces or be hiding in London. If he has killed himself he is probably not far from Park Farm, and the police dragged ponds with that idea.

Rather to my surprise Holmes made no comment or any sort of interruption to my reading of the newspaper piece. Rather was he rapt with attention throughout my narration. Then, when I had lowered the newspaper he said, 'Upon my word, what a lurid story. So the murderer, as they already refer to him, without trial or really thorough investigation, made off from the scene of the assault, discarding axes, razors and a revolver, and still having another pistol about him. He certainly went into that parlour well armed, and left it, having discarded one revolver, waving another! (For how else were they aware that he had it?) I tell you, Watson, the poor fellow has been tried and all but sentenced to death by the *Daily Mirror*. Local people in Finchley may well get up a lynch mob when they read it!'

I was rather surprised at Holmes's reaction, for all of my sympathies were with the brave old showman who had been butchered, and I said as much.

Holmes's response was even more surprising to me. 'Watson, examine some of the wild statements quoted. Why, there is even an admission that some statements are based on rumour, which as you know can be a lying jade. Standing on the saddle of his bicycle and walking on his hands sound rather like quite normal activities for a young man, especially if there were ladies about. Lord George said himself that Cooper was a good worker, and had made him his valet at one point, and got him off a police charge when he chased some trespassers off Sanger's land, probably on his master's orders. But then we will have to question Jackson, Austin and anyone else we can find at Park Farm for ourselves to get to the truth. Cooper's father is there too and might shed some light.'

I started, 'You mean that you are going to Finchley? Why, I thought you had retired years ago?'

He nodded, 'Yes, but the death of George Sanger involves unfinished business from a decade ago, Watson. Perhaps you would be good enough to look up the trains from Brighton to Victoria whilst I prepare for the journey. We will read any other newspaper accounts that we can find during the journey. Come, it will be a pleasant interlude I feel sure, despite its tragic cause.'

Had I been told a few hours earlier that 'The Game Would Be Afoot' I would have disbelieved the speaker, yet here I was, embarking upon an exploit, adventure or case, call it what you will. But of course, as my friend had pointed out to me, it was really perhaps part of some unfinished business.

We found a first-class smoker and settled down to the important job of reading anything that we could find in the newspapers concerning the Sanger tragedy. Unfortunately the more respectful dailies had very little information, making no accusations and just giving a rather less lurid picture of the tragedy than the one I had read aloud to Holmes and from which I had gained a mental picture of poor old Sanger lying with his skull split and making his dying depositions!

At Victoria Station we saw news placards bearing slogans such as 'Lord of the Circus Slain . . . by Mad Axe-Man!'

Holmes grunted and said, 'Well, well, Watson, Cooper has already been promoted to become a mad axe-man!'

It took us longer to reach Park Farm, Finchley, by cab from Victoria than it had taken to reach that station from Brighton, but at last around three of the clock we were looking at the impressive exterior of Sanger's farmhouse. It really was most impressive too, the entrance to the old showman's Xanadu. The main portion of the house, ivy-clad and dark of brick, was formed by three large sections, each with a bay window and with a recessed portion between each of these. Over the impressive canopied entrance was a coat of arms from Astley's, doubtless rescued from the demolition of some twenty years earlier. At one end of the building was a red-tiled extension barn, probably added at the time of Sanger's earlier occupation, to house his parade wagons or animal cages.

This house formed the south wall of a quadrant of buildings, all but enclosing a pleasant lawn which was protected by sections of fence. In the centre of this lawn stood a plinth, which supported a truly enormous animal skull which proved to be that of an elephant, despite a lack of tusks which had at first made me think that it was the head of some great whale. Ducks and chickens wandered around at will, though they seemed somewhat disturbed by the large number of sightseers through whom we had to push our way in order to gain the entrance to the house. This was guarded by a uniformed police officer who demanded to know what business brought us to the scene of the tragedy.

My friend said, 'I am Sherlock Holmes and this is my friend and colleague, Dr John Watson. As to our business here . . .'

But the policeman saluted and stood aside, saying, 'I reckon they will be glad of your help in there, Mr Holmes.

I remember you well; back in Inspector Lestrade's days it was when I last saw you. Well, old George has retired now, but you will find that Detective Sergeant Colman is a bright enough fellow. Chief Inspector Kane is in charge of the case, but he is off searching for Cooper at present.'

Inside the entrance was imposingly lined with examples of the taxidermist's art; in my ignorance I would have referred to them as stuffed animals. There were tigers, bears, monkeys and even the head of an Asiatic elephant with a large scar between its eyes. I had seen an animal stuffed upon one occasion when in Afghanistan. I explained to Holmes how this was done by skinning the animal, preserving its hide then cleaning the skeleton to use as a base with padding to replace the flesh.

Holmes nodded and said, 'But not in this case, Watson, for the creature's skull is on display outside upon a plinth.'

I rounded on him. 'How do you know that it is not the skull of a different elephant?'

He smiled and replied, 'Because there is a bullet hole in the skull which exactly corresponds with the scar upon this head. The tusks are missing from the skull, because they are here, fixed into the sockets by doubtless ingenious means.'

Detective Sergeant Colman was, I suppose, a nice enough young man, yet there was something in his manner which whilst not insolent was somewhat patronizing. He said, 'Sherlock Holmes, eh? My word, there is a name from the past! Old Lestrade often amuses his cronies at reunions with tales of his adventures in your company, sir, but you will find that our methods have changed a good deal since your time.'

I was furious but Holmes remained very calm indeed.

He filled his pipe from his pocket pouch, studying Colman as he did so. Then, when he had struck a vesta and produced a cloud of blue smoke, remarked, 'Yet despite your up-to-date ideas you still favour an age-old breed of dog for a companion; the Irish wolfhound is an admirable creature, though I am not fond of dogs myself. I feel sure that having been summoned to this case quite suddenly but at a very early hour you have made considerable progress already. I observe that you had a very late night due to your enrolment as a member of some secret order; perhaps some police version of the masonic movement?'

There was a silence that you could have cut with a knife; then Colman gasped, 'How could you have known these things? We have never met before.' Then a glimmer of understanding crossed his honest enough face and he said, 'I suppose Constable Arkright, on guard at the door, has been opening his large mouth; though how he could have known these things is beyond me!'

Holmes smiled, kindly. 'I would hardly have pumped your policeman, neither would I have had the need to, my dear Colman, for these things are obvious to those who observe and interpret that which they see. Your dog is a large one, it leaves its hairs only upon your clothes above waist level. There is, though, in any case no mistaking those harsh grizzled hairs of a wolfhound. Had you had time on your side when you left home you would have caused these hairs to be removed.'

The detective grunted and said, 'Yes, but how about the part concerning the secret society? Come, sir, this you could not have known without being informed by someone!'

My friend struck another vesta, for his pipe was temperamental, and replied, 'Well, I can tell that you had little sleep from the puffy nature of the delicate sacs beneath your eyes. By the way, that is, I am happy to inform you, a temporary symptom and a good night's sleep will restore the elasticity. I assumed that you had been involved in some sort of initiation ceremony from the concertina-like appearance of the left leg of your breeches. Again, had you not left home in a great hurry this morning you would have got the garment pressed or sorted out another pair.'

Of course, Colman said, 'I see. All obvious when you come to think about it.' Even so he treated Holmes with some sort of respect from that time on.

At the far end of the entrance hall there was an oak-panelled door which Colman told us was the Parlour or the scene of the crime. This door was firmly closed and we were told that it was locked and that even we were not permitted to enter this room. Yet enter it we did, under rather bizarre circumstances. It happened this way: quite suddenly a high-pitched voice, rather like that of an elderly woman, was heard from behind the locked door. The voice, as far as I could hear it, was shouting, 'George!' and 'Where's George?' in turn.

Colman started. 'That room is locked and there was no one in there when it was secured. The windows are fastened too, I cannot see how anyone can be in there!'

Yet again, the voice insisted upon asking, 'George . . . where's George?'

Colman collected himself and reached into a police satchel for the door key which he produced eventually and unfastened the door, throwing it open. We entered the room, a comfortably furnished apartment with old-fashioned sofas and chairs lining its walls. But there was no person within.

Yet again the voice was heard, much louder and more shrill. 'Where's George?'

Then Colman laughed and said, 'No ghost, gentlemen, just a parrot!'

Holmes, who had seemed unsurprised by the whole episode, corrected him. 'It is a macaw, very like a parrot but much larger. Notice the beauty of its plumes which will possibly be the undoing of its species.'

The beautiful great parrot-like bird moved its head up and down as it stood upon the perch in the corner. It had no leg chain, being obviously an extremely well-trained and trusted pet. Colman moved to the door and called,

'Someone collect this poor bird. It doubtless needs feeding!'

As he did so I asked Holmes, very quietly, 'You were not surprised when we found the bird was the source of the vocalistics?'

He smiled. 'Not in the least, for these creatures, although wonderful mimics, have tones unmistakable to the trained ear.'

I said, 'Why then did you not tell Colman that it was a macaw?'

He replied, 'Because, Watson, I had wanted to see the inside of this room. I doubt if he will turf us out of it now.'

A young man entered the room and held out an arm, onto which the macaw leapt and perched quite comfortably. He was a man of about five and twenty, neatly dressed, with the oiled quiff and waxed moustache dictated by fashion.

The bird cried, 'Where's George?' for the twelfth or fourteenth time.

The young man seemed saddened by this utterance. He said, 'Sorry, gentlemen, I'll take this fellow to another room and attend to his needs. He was a great favourite of Lord George's, and will miss him, poor old chap. So will I, for that matter. I'm Jackson, Lord George's valet.'

Colman was occupied outside the room with some police routine and Holmes took advantage of this to ask Jackson some questions, first telling him his identity and mine. He asked, 'You were in this room when Sanger was attacked by Cooper, the so-called mad axe-man?'

Jackson smiled wearily. 'I would hardly call him that, Mr Holmes, and I was the one he attacked. It was this way. We were both sitting in this room, the guv'nor and myself. I was reading to the old man when Cooper burst in the room and brandished an axe at me. But he brought it only onto the pad of my jacket shoulder and I don't believe me meant me any real damage with it.'

Holmes's eyes narrowed. 'What makes you say that?'

He replied, 'Well, it is not as if he came into the house armed with the axe, for it was the one which was kept in the elephant's foot in the lobby, in case it was needed for the firewood. Evidently in his temper he grabbed it on his way in. But, as I have said, he did not brandish it with any real power; ruined my best suit, but that was all.'

I enquired, 'But the newspaper reports inferred that it was Sanger that he attacked.'

Jackson shook his head. 'It was me he wanted to punish; Lord George just got in his way when he got up from his chair and grabbed the candelabrum. He made to strike Cooper with it. He was a game old man, but Cooper was a strong lad. Even so, he did little more than give the guv'nor a shove, back into his chair. Unfortunately, Lord George banged his head on the candleabrum, but it only brought up a small bruise; I didn't think he was seriously hurt.'

Holmes was deeply interested now. He enquired, 'What next occurred, Mr Jackson?'

The valet said, 'Well, Cooper had dropped the axe and made no effort to retrieve it when Mr Austin, he was a trusted retainer from Sanger's circus days, entered the room and sized up the situation and made towards Cooper, doubtless merely to put him out of the room. But Cooper lost his head and grabbed the open razor off the mantelpiece and brandished it. Austin tried to grab him and he got a small cut on his face before Cooper dropped it. You see, sir, again there was no intent to hurt Austin; he grabbed the razor, I think, as an automatic gesture of defence. Then he made a run for it out of the building. We chased him, Austin and I, also purely as a token gesture for I for one felt it best to let him get well away and calm himself. He wasn't a bad sort of chap and I can well understand his jealousy concerning myself. The old man made quite a lot of him for a year or more, taking him everywhere, letting him valet for him and even hinting concerning his will. Then a week or two back he started to act strangely towards the lad, accusing him of stealing fifty pounds from his desk; which I'm sure he did not do; and also hinted that Cooper had something to do with a dozen horses that had gone missing. Cooper offered to go to the police over these things, but Sanger refused to make official accusations.'

I felt sure that all of this was extremely interesting to Holmes, but I could see that he wanted to learn as much from Jackson as he could before the sergeant returned. He asked, with some sense of urgency, 'So did old Sanger accompany you out of the building?'

He replied, 'No, sir, he stayed put, wisely in his chair. He was not much hurt but he was a very old man.'

Holmes chuckled. 'So much for the press account of Sanger lying insensible and mortally wounded outside the house!'

Colman returned to the room and looked suspiciously around at us. 'You shouldn't be in here you know, any of you. Mr Jackson, please take that bird away!'

Jackson grinned at us and left the room, with the macaw again yelling, 'Where's George?'

We made to leave the room also but Colman relented, saying, 'You can stay and look around if you wish, so long as you don't touch anything.'

Holmes nodded and said, 'My thanks, Sergeant, and I wonder if I might see the razor, the axe and the revolver, the one discarded by Cooper when he escaped?'

Colman replied, 'See no reason why not.' He lifted a cardboard box from a side table and placed it upon a footstool opening the lid for us to see inside. The axe looked like any other but the revolver interested me. I said, 'That is surely a collector's piece, I doubt if it would even fire.'

But Holmes was more interested in the razor. It was, as had been reported in the press, adapted to stay permanently open. 'You will observe the wooden splint tied tightly by twine to the handle making the blade quite immovable. Do you really believe, as the press evidently do, that he was carrying this implement about his person?'

Colman was puzzled. 'Why not, Holmes?'

The detective late of Baker Street and more recently

from Fowlhaven said, 'If you were going to set out to do murder with a razor would you not be sure that it would fold and close lest it damaged your own person before doing harm to others? This razor has been adapted for a certain purpose, possibly, as this is a farm, of a veterinary nature. As for the axe, I have learned that this was kept amid umbrellas and canes in the elephant foot, immediately inside the front door, and Cooper doubtless picked it up on his way in as an afterthought. Finally, we come to the revolver. This is a theatrical piece, built to fire blank cartridges. Examine it yourself and you will find this is so, for I'll wager it is loaded with blanks if it is loaded at all.'

Holmes turned away and studied the wall over the mantelpiece as Colman carefully examined the revolver. The sergeant said, 'Well I'm blessed, you are right, for once (I blanched at these words), it is little more than an ornate starting pistol.'

Holmes turned to face him and pointed dramatically at the wall. 'Do you see its scarred outline on the wallpaper. There are two nails which would have supported it, if rather gingerly. There are other firearms on display. Perhaps we could talk to Mr Austin, with your kind permission.'

Colman looked thoughtful. 'See no harm in it. I'll send for him.'

Harry Austin was an athlete in figure but a funster by facial expression and construction. He had that elongated chin and broad grin ever associated with clowns. I remembered him vaguely from our contacts with Sanger of some years before; indeed as part of an equestrian act 'The Brothers Austin'. He remembered us well and displayed that memory so often to be found among circus and theatre folk.

He seemed pleased to see us and, pleasantries over, he

answered our questions. 'Yes, I agree with Jackson's comments. There was no real harm in Cooper and the old man had indeed ill used him. As for the razor, the old man kept it on the mantlepiece for doctoring his pets, such as the macaw and the monkeys (which he could not bear to part with at the sale) and he would pare claws with it and so on. It was fixed open with a wooden splint since he once cut himself badly when cauterizing an ulcer on one of the dogs. The pistol? Why, that was used in Mazeppa, when it was enacted in the circus. It would only fire blanks.'

Holmes asked, 'Did you have reason to believe that he was carrying another revolver?'

Austin said, 'No, but I suppose he could have been. That one fell off the wall during the struggle.'

Harry Austin offered to show us over the farm, and Colman, possibly glad enough to be rid of us, consented that we might be escorted around. His last words to us for that time, 'Be sure not to interfere with anything, leave the real detective work to the professionals!'

Immediately behind the house there were the usual farm barns and buildings and in the distance could be seen fields with cattle and horses grazing. About fifty feet from the house but well short of these fields there stood a familiar sight to us both, it was the Vardo, as Lord George had always referred to that which I would have called a caravan. It was just as we remembered it, with its highly polished brasswork and neatly curtained windows. How often I had seen Lord George sitting upon its steps, surveying his tober with a critical eye.

Austin told us that the old showman had quite often slept in the wagon, finding it sometimes hard to sleep in a house. I pointed to a large shed, or small wooden barn one could have called it. I enquired, 'Is that for storage?'

But Austin shook his head, 'The guv'nor rented it to a sort of mad-hat inventor; goodness knows why, for he didn't need the money. Herr Klauk his name is. Want to meet him?'

Holmes nodded, and Austin took us over to the big sectional building. There was a notice, PRIVATE. KEEP AWAY, but Austin disregarded it and thumped upon the door. Some banging from within ceased and eventually the door opened to reveal a short stockily-built gentleman of Teutonic appearance, complete with cropped hair and shaved neck.

He spoke in guttural tones. 'What is it, what do you want? Oh, it is you Herr Harry!'

Austin introduced us to Klauk, who let us into his huge workshop with good enough grace. There were various tools upon carpenter's benches and larger pieces of machinery hanging from walls. But at the end of the building, propped up on wooden supports, stood what looked for all the world like a huge silver sausage. It was in fact a scale model of an airship; the kind that has a basket underneath for passengers or goods. But the small scale of this particular airship would have made it unsuitable to transport persons other than a troupe of Sanger's midgets! Herr Klauk was extremely friendly despite the menace of the notice on the barn door but many years of association with Sherlock Holmes told me that he had been alerted to some kind of suspicion. This, however, he made no display of and I feel sure that his thoughts would not have been detected by anyone save myself. In retrospect I have often wondered if Klauk's experiments had any connection with the eventual dropping of deadly cargoes of explosives from airships on a much larger scale onto the largest city in the world.

These silvery harbingers of death and destruction would, in the early years of the Great War, be referred to as Zeppelins, but such ghastly experiences were at that time nearly half a decade into the future. All the same, I have never discussed the matter with Holmes and I must remember to do so next time I visit him at Fowlhaven. I would be interested to know if he had suspicion of experimentation which would not have been in our country's interest and if so had he conveyed such fears to the British government, or at least those departments concerned with espionage.

But we were at that time concerned more with the Sanger tragedy and information concerning the unfortunate and unwise youth, Cooper.

Klauk was loquacious enough upon the subject. 'Yes, I knew Herbert quite well. When I first came here he used to tell me of the grand adventures that he had when accompanying his master upon expeditions to the city, or Petticoat Lane. He would say when being greeted by the delighted traders, "You see, Herbert, these are my people and it is good to be among them again." '

Holmes interrupted, 'I am more interested in the rift between Sanger and Cooper which several people have inferred.'

Klauk said, 'Herr Austin may remember the incident of the missing horses. Sanger declared that twelve horses had been taken from his meadow and he seemed to infer that someone close to him was responsible for their theft.'

Austin nodded. 'Cooper suggested that he should go to the police about it, but he refused to do so and forbade us all, my wife, myself, Jackson and Herr Klauk being the only persons knowing about it.'

Klauk nodded and said, 'Then there was the matter of the fifty pounds which the old man claimed to be missing from his desk in the parlour. He would keep on about it, even when others were present, saying to Cooper, "I've an idea which young fellow has taken it and I will have to do something about it." But Cooper's response seemed to take the wind out of his sails, for the lad said, "I didn't take your money, guv'nor, and I am tired of your insinuations. I'm going to the police about it, to tell them what you have said to me." At that Sanger got angry, saying that if he did he would deny the loss of the fifty pounds. After that he didn't want to have Cooper about him and started to take Jackson into his confidence, making him his valet in place of Cooper who was banished from the house.'

I asked, 'Was he dismissed?'

Austin said, 'No, but he was forced to sleep in a barn, to which he took his things. He remained respectful, but I could tell he was seething with anger.'

The German inventor looked thoughtful. 'He was always asking me about my years in Paris; I resided there for quite a long time; I used to regale him with stories of my Parisian adventures and he would say, "If only I could learn a bit of French." He was extremely strong you know. At the far end of this shed there is a sliding door for taking my model onto the meadow. Normally it would take two people to pull it across, but Cooper could do it alone.'

He paused, then added, 'Sanger had told him a good deal about Paris too, for he had visited the French capital on a number of occasions. But of course that was back when the old man was still amiable towards him.'

We thanked Klauk for his time and information, departing to continue the tour of Park Farm. Harry Austin, whilst showing us the cattle byre, told us that he was married to Ellen, grand-daughter of Lord George Sanger; so he was no mere employee. Eventually we told him that we could not fairly take up more of his time. He took the hint with extreme politeness and returned to the house.

We sat upon the steps of Sanger's living wagon and discussed that which we had learned. Holmes took out his pipe and discovered that he was without more than a pinch of the Scottish mixture. I let him have some of my tobacco but he found it somewhat mild. He was therefore somewhat irritable during our conversation.

I said, 'So Cooper has enormous strength and has delusions of grandeur and bore a grudge against Sanger.'

Holmes puffed away at the, to him, unsatisfying stimulant. 'Watson, we have indeed learned that he was strong, a bit of a dandy, prone to show off his abilities. He also longed to visit exciting-sounding faraway places. In other words he is a perfectly normal young man who has been pushed to the edge of his patience through his employers', probably, false accusations. His behaviour during the incident which led, perhaps indirectly, to Sanger's death makes him seem to me to be very restrained and far from being the mad axe-man of accusation. When he entered the house to confront Sanger he brought no weapons with him and brandished only those which he discovered. Even then he showed remarkable restraint considering the mood that he must have been in. The damage to Sanger's forehead was accidental, and all but self-inflicted.'

I enquired, 'Shall you help Colman and his chief inspector, whom we have not as yet met?'

Holmes considered. 'If they will allow it, which I rather doubt. We are not dealing with a Lestrade or Gregson, both of whom knew my abilities had some pedigree, despite their dubiety.'

I understood his train of thought but, sensing his mood, did not press him further. We made to return to the house but encountered one of the milkmaids near the back door. She said, in a strong Hertfordshire tone, 'Ooh, sirs, can you tell me what is happening inside?'

We told her what we could and what was wise to impart. Holmes asked her name and she said, 'Flossie, sir. I was friendly with Bertie Cooper. He's a nice fellow is Bertie, ambitious and smart, not like the local lads at all.'

She glanced downwards sheepishly and I surmised that she was somewhat smitten with Herbert Cooper.

Holmes asked her, 'Flossie, where do you suppose Bertie to have gone? If I can find him I might be able to save him from serious charges, for he is not a bad sort of chap from what I have learned.'

She said, 'Sir, you are right. Lord George used him ill and had no right to accuse him of things without proof. The last I saw of him he was disappearing upon his bicycle and shouting "Flossie, God bless you. I must go to the railway!" '

Holmes seemed interested in this last remark and enquired of her, 'Pray what did you make of that?'

She said, 'Why, sir, I imagined he was going to get a train that would set him on the way to those faraway places he had said so much about.' The detective patted her arm, nodded and we re-entered the house.

Back in the lobby we found Chief Inspector Kane had returned and we were introduced to him by Colman. But where Colman had been a touch patronizing Kane was downright uncouth; at least such was my impression of him. He said, 'Sherlock Holmes, why I thought the name to be that of a fictional character whose exploits appear in a monthly magazine, mainly confined to dentists' waiting rooms? For instance, there are accounts of your deducing correctly a man's occupation and recent activities just by observation. This insults my intellect and whoever writes up such trash needs something better to do. Detective work these days is scientific, plus a great deal of hard work. We don't sit around surrounded by clouds of tobacco smoke, playing a violin and writing monographs. Moreover, we certainly do not get up in disguise and sneak about on the moors or anything like that. I do not read such stuff as your friend's chronicles of your exploits.'

Holmes smiled engagingly and said, 'If that is your rule you have broken it three or four times, Inspector. You are obviously familiar with several of my characteristics, which are not together described in any one episode. Moreover, you are also familiar with certain events which occur quite well into the serial account of *The Hound of the Baskervilles*.'

Kane grunted. 'Very well, you've made your point. Perhaps I have glanced at a few of the episodes. But that does not make their content any more believable. Those deductions that I mentioned for example . . . what can you tell me concerning my own exploits, recent ones for instance?'

Holmes became ever so slightly assertive. 'Well, for one thing you have broken your golden rule and have been to Victoria Station to watch the boat train, in disguise!'

Kane boomed, 'Wrong. I was not in disguise!'

My friend retorted, 'You are a policeman, yet you stood there in ordinary attire and not in a policeman's uniform.'

Kane scoffed, 'You play with words, you don't even know

for certain that I went to Victoria rather than Charing Cross.'

'Elementary, my dear Inspector. The road is up in front of the station, as I noticed when I travelled here from Fowlhaven by way of Brighton. A chalk dust of a kind which I have not encountered before had been disturbed.'

Kane snapped, 'What kind of texture does it have?'

Sherlock Holmes pointed to the inspector's boots and said, quietly, 'There is a goodly amount of it upon your footwear still, so I suggest you examine it, even scientifically. In any case I back this deduction with a leaflet which protrudes from your side greatcoat pocket, giving times of boat trains between Victoria and various locations, including Paris.'

Kane, far from showing any kind of good grace, snarled, 'Well, if you are so clever why don't you find the mad axeman for me?' Holmes smiled politely and made to leave the house by the front entrance.

I paused before following to enquire, 'We have your permission to investigate upon your behalf?'

The inspector shrugged and said, 'Why not? Cooper has left the country by now, so have a good trip!'

Outside I said, 'Holmes, he is likely to be right. After all, a witness said that he was seen riding his bicycle in the direction of the railway, and Flossie said that his last words to her were "I must go to the railway"! We have no idea where to begin to look.'

Holmes grunted and blew noisily through his empty pipe. 'You may have no idea, Watson, but that does not mean that I do not.'

Absence of nicotine was making him crusty as he banged the pipe upon a post. 'I must first buy some tobacco, Watson, for I cannot operate without it.' As he spoke, a small dog of the terrier breed appeared, and started to jump up at my friend, doubtless with friendly enough intent. But Holmes is no dog lover and demanded, 'Capture the brute. He annoys me!'

I caught the lively little creature by its collar, and it continued to gyrate and try to leap about. Then the milkmaid Flossie appeared, saying apologetically, 'Oh, sir, that's Bertie's dog, Julie. He thinks the world of her, and she of him. She has been inconsolable with his going so you must forgive her.'

What Holmes said next amazed me, in light of what he had recently opined. 'Please think nothing of it; of course the poor little creature must be sad without her master. May we perhaps take her for a stroll down the lane?'

Flossie clapped her hands and said, 'Oh, sir, how kind. I can tell you are fond of dogs; just wait while I get her lead!'

Flossie skipped off, greatly pleased by Holmes's 'kindness'. I said, 'I realize, Holmes, that you have some ulterior motive, though what it is I cannot think for the life of me!'

Sherlock placed a finger to his lips as the girl returned with the leather thong which she clipped to Julie's collar. We set forth, with Holmes holding the lead and wearing a fixed grin, until we were out of sight of the house.

Once we had reached the lane and were walking towards the railway, which our cab had passed only hours before, Holmes said, 'The dog could be useful, Watson. See, she has a good nose which I observe by the way she sniffs at the grass. The girl said that Cooper spoke of going to the railway; but made no mention of a station which he might well have done had he been making for it. If we take this next turning we should strike the nearest point of the railway line to Park Farm.'

I was bewildered. 'Why would he want the line rather than the station? He could only go abroad by boarding a train to Victoria or Charing Cross.'

Holmes replied, 'He may have had no such intent.'

We gained a point where the line was actually in distant sight and as we made for the railway embankment Holmes said, loudly, 'Where's Bertie . . . Bertie! Where is Bertie?' The dog pricked its ears and sniffed the air, then made towards the line. But Holmes, to my complete surprise, checked the dog and took a right turning along the lane, dragging the protesting terrier. I asked, 'Holmes, why on earth are you deliberately going against the dog's clear indication?' But I needed no answer as I saw the tobacconist's shop. Holmes entered and purchased two ounces of Scottish mixture which he quickly transferred from its newspaper cone to his pouch, and then a goodly portion to the bowl of his pipe. He lit it and closed his eyes at the ecstasy of a lungful of heavy smoke. Then he smiled blissfully and repeated his words to the dog. This time he followed it, and I him.

As we neared the edge of the railway embankment we peered over the wooded rim to the railway line below. The embankment was neither high nor steep, or not extremely so. We climbed up fairly easily and scanned the line in both directions. Holmes appealed to the dog again and we followed its excited bounds and short excursions into the undergrowth on the slopes. At last the dog stopped, its nose twitching and uttering some rather wheezy grunts. She suddenly darted into the bracken and looked back at us with an 'I've found something' expression on her intense little face. Holmes probed with his ashplant and I prodded around also with my cane. All we found were the ashes from a fire and a depression in the grass, denoting the laying down of an animal or person. I asked, 'Do you think he could have lain here overnight?'

Holmes said, 'It could be where a tramp has lain, but I have hopes, Watson, I have hopes. If he was indeed here, he has not long left, for the ashes are fresh and although not warm their feel is not as cold as it would be after more than a few hours. If Cooper slept here he may not yet be too far away.'

Julie sniffed at the indentation made by several hours of pressure from a body and then showed signs of wishing to continue. Holmes said, 'Find Bertie!' and let go of the lead. To me he said, 'I have no wish to cramp the animal's activity. If she finds Cooper we will soon know.' He sat upon the bank and gratefully smoked a pipe of the Scottish mixture.

Within a few minutes there was a heart-rending howl, which inferred that Julie could have found her beloved master. She continued to howl and we followed the sound which led us round a bend in the track.

We found there not just the dog but one of the most terrifyingly horrific sights that I have ever experienced, and I am a medical man! On the middle of the track, between the lines lay a man's head. Between one of the lines and the embankment lay what had to be the body of the same individual. Dear reader, the sight of a headless body is horrendous, but a bodiless head is more so, and we had found both. Holmes seemed unaffected as he knelt to examine first the head. It was grossly disfigured on one side, but as Holmes gently turned it over it was clearly that of Cooper, from the appearance of its right side, if descriptions were anything to go by. There was half of a waxed moustache, and some blood-clotted hair arranged in what might have been an oiled quiff.

I examined the body as best I could and had to agree with Holmes that Cooper — for we felt certain that this was he — had taken his own life by laying his neck upon one of the railway lines. A train had gone over his neck completely severing it from his body, and recently at that from the state of the blood and the fact that rigor mortis had scarcely begun to set in. Holmes had evidently deduced this without examining the body as I did. He said, 'This is recent, Watson; the engine driver could well have missed the fact that he had taken his great spluttering monster over Cooper, especially in the half light of the morning. But the gang of wheeltappers, and other workmen who would daily pass along this line, could scarce miss it. Please be good enough to fetch Kane and Colman, and in so doing please take this wretched dog with you, for its howling is getting upon my nerves!'

Julie was very difficult to remove from the scene of grizzly carnage, but I did manage to get the heartbroken dog away from the grossly ungrateful detective, though she lagged and made my progress very slow.

I hate to be the bearer of bad news and I delivered Julie to the milkmaid who collapsed in a flood of tears. I calmed her as best I could and then hastened to inform Chief Inspector Kane regarding our awful discovery. He and Colman were seated in the parlour where Austin and his wife, who I now knew to be Sanger's grand-daughter, were dispensing coffee.

'What?' Kane leapt to his feet and although I should

imagine he was relieved to have his missing fugitive found there was yet a hint of annoyance that it was Sherlock Holmes who was responsible for the discovery. He yelled, 'Colman, take a constable and organize some conveyance to take the body to the police mortuary. That is, if you can be sure that it is in fact Cooper.'

I had scarce time to gulp down some hot coffee before it was time for me to return to the railway, this time in a police gig with Kane. I had given Colman precise directions as to where to find the body, thoughtfully resisting the temptation to tell him to take and follow the dog. When we got to the mournful scene I found Colman inspecting the body whilst Holmes sat upon a mound smoking his pipe. Kane nodded curtly to Holmes and then conversed with the constable who had been first on the scene.

The body, and the head, were soon being prepared by police medical staff for removal. As soon as he realized that this was about to happen Holmes spoke to Kane upon the matter for the first time. 'Chief Inspector, would this not be a good moment for you to search the body for anything the man Cooper was carrying which could become lost or dislodged by these activities?'

Kane glowered at him. 'When I want your advice, Mr Amateur Detective, I will ask for it!' All the same, after a moment's thought he ordered Colman to search the clothing on Cooper's body.

As the detective sergeant placed a number of objects into a large official police envelope he kept aside what appeared to be a letter, although it had no envelope. Kane enquired, 'What is it, a suicide note?'

Colman replied, 'Well, yes and no. It appears to be a letter written to Cooper's father . . .'

He tailed off and Kane stamped his foot with impatience, saying, 'Well read it out, lad!'

Colman read the letter so that we all could hear . . . .

Dear Father,

Something bad has happened. They say I did it but I don't remember any such thing. All I recall is loud voices and then I ran away.

The guv'nor turned against me, after my six years of faithful service to him, accusing me of stealing from him and other things too. There was a matter of fifty pounds missing, but I know now that he lodged it behind his dressing mirror. In his desk will be found a paper referring to those horses that were supposed to have been stolen.

Those women had it in for me and turned him against me. But God forgive me for the wrong I have done, even so. Hope you will forgive me too.

Goodbye, Father. Also Len, Dick and Tom.

Your broken-hearted son,

Herbert.

Kane allowed us at least a sight of the letter and then placed it into the envelope, saying, 'Well, Mr Detective, what do you deduce from the letter other than the fact that he did not have a stamp or an envelope?'

Holmes smiled with false politeness and said, 'Not much, except that he wrote part of the letter at the farm and finished it shortly before his demise.'

Kane looked at him with a sideways, rather guarded, look. 'What makes you think that?'

Holmes said, 'The front of the sheet is written in ink, with a waverley nib. The other side of the paper finishes the letter in pencil. He had no writing materials with him, but I'll wager you have found a soft pencil about his person.

Obviously he left Park Farm suddenly, it being inconvenient for him to finish the letter he was writing. By the way, have you found the famous revolver?'

It was Colman who made the peace by saying, 'No, just a gold watch and eighteen shillings in change.'

But Kane growled, 'That is not to say that he did not throw the revolver away. Possibly a search of the surrounding undergrowth might yield it up.'

Holmes was ironic, 'Chief Inspector, why not drag the Thames at Westminster for it?'

Kane started. 'Why should we do that?'

Sherlock Holmes replied, 'Because you would have as much chance of finding it there as in the undergrowth on the bank, because I for one do not believe that it exists. The man went into the farmhouse unarmed and left it the same way.'

The senior police detective glared at Holmes. 'What about the axe, the razor and the other revolver?'

Holmes said, 'All were at the scene of the tragedy, and whilst the axe and the razor were brandished they do not really figure in the crime, so-called, and as for the other pistol, as you call it, that fell from the wall and did not come into the incident at all.'

The body was taken by police ambulance to the mortuary and I wondered if Holmes would wish to follow it for further investigation but quietly he said to me, 'Watson, I think we will return to Park Farm where the pressure will be off now that Cooper has been found. Clearly he has taken his own life and we can learn little more from the poor fellow's body.'

We strolled back to Park Farm at a slow pace. We had planned to spend the night at a local hostelry, but Harry

Austin had extended an invitation for us to stay at the farmhouse; we decided to accept this kind offer of hospitality.

Back at the farmhouse we were given a more than satisfying meal by Mrs Austin, whom we had not met before. But then she was Sanger's grand-daughter and had possibly been prostrated by grief. For this reason we were very careful not to upset her by any word or deed. I estimated that Ellen Austin was a woman in her mid-thirties, small, dark and with the same pronounced cheekbones of her grandfather. She was attired in black. The domestic arrangements being at sixes and sevens owing to the tragic events of the past forty-eight hours there was no official dinner, meals being prepared as and when and for whomsoever needed. But the Austins joined us in the drawing-room after we had eaten; the parlour being naturally out of use.

She said, 'It is going to be very strange here without granddad; he was a very strong character you know.' We agreed and told her something of our contact with him of a decade before. She continued, 'He trusted people far too much and they would take advantage of that trust. Herbert Cooper is the last and tragic example of it. You know, grandad thought the world of that boy, taking him everywhere and trusting him enough to make him into his companion on account of Harry and I having so much to do running this household. All he had to do was look after grandad's clothes and read to him in the evenings sometimes.' She paused, as if she felt that she had said something unwise, but recovered quickly and continued, 'Grandad was eighty-four and he had trouble reading on account of his eyes.'

Holmes enquired gently, 'There had been other valet companions had there not?'

She nodded. 'Yes, but they always seemed to steal from him or take advantage of him sooner or later. Jackson seemed to be satisfactory, but who knows how he would have turned out after a year or so? As it is we will never know.' Harry Austin seemed a little dismayed by his wife's little outburst, but said little. Holmes and I exchanged a glance, which from long association told us that we agreed that the time was hardly right to press certain questions.

There were twenty bedrooms at Park Farm, so there was little difficulty for the Austins to find us a couple of tolerably comfortable rooms. We were shown the ornate panelled door which was the entrance to the bedroom of Lord George where he had been laid out by a local woman who specialized in such duties. As we tiptoed reverently past the room, Harry Austin whispered, 'Ellen renewed his rouge and some gyp on his hair and beard, as I'm sure he would have wished. There will be an inquest later, but we have been given permission to go ahead with the funeral.'

# IV

# The Secrets of the Vardo

I would like to be able to tell the reader that the day of Lord George Sanger's funeral dawned bright with autumnal sunshine and crisp November brightness. But, alas, I can say no such thing. The day was one of pouring rain and gusty wind which did little to improve Holmes's temper; for he was suffering from an autumn malady, a severe chill which threatened to extend to bronchitis. It had been with him for a day or two and his coughing was awful to hear, and as a medical man I was forced to advise him to cease the use of strong tobacco for a few days but of course he would not co-operate. Indeed he would not even allow me to minister to him, saying frequently, 'Do not fuss, Watson. You sound like an old woman!'

But when he seemed determined to follow the cortège to Margate, where Lord George was to be interred, I felt forced to put my foot down. 'Holmes, if you go out in this weather I will not answer for the consequences; you could get pneumonia. I will represent us both and you can spend a quiet day here, recovering. I feel sure that the Austins would also be grateful for your presence here too, for most of the servants will be going to Margate and there will be no other responsible person on the spot.

Much to my surprise, Holmes needed little encouragement to take my advice and stay in almost sole charge of Park Farm. But he insisted in coming out in the hallway, draped in a shawl to stand, head bowed as Sanger's handsome sarcophagus was carried to the hearse. An incredible number of local people had gathered to see the cortège off from the farmhouse, on its journey to the main-line station that Sanger might be conveyed to Margate. The coffin was completely obscured by wreaths and flowers, which spilled over into a second horse-drawn carriage. They were from the Fossetts, the Pinders, the Yeldings, the Ginnets, the Bakers, and a dozen other circus families and their many branches. Larger tributes came from the Showman's Guild and other societies.

The Riderless Horse is of course an old tradition among equestrian family funerals. At Sanger's there were two milk-white steeds, part of the Sanger stud, which looked very dramatic and gained gasps from the very large crowd of onlookers. The cavalcade proceeded to the railway, seeming for all the world like one of Sanger's own circus parades, with its many horse-drawn equipages. The route was lined with bare-headed rustics showing their respect. But these scenes of respectful interest could hardly prepare me for the display of public concern which awaited us at Margate. After all, Lord George owned there several theatres, shops, the zoo and a huge amusement park. He was, in fact, almost Lord Margate, being a very important representative upon various local committees of local governors and tradesfolk. As the cortège and its followers made the slow progress towards the cemetery the same scene was repeated with almost every street lined with mourners. The rain was relentless and the sight of so many black umbrellas everywhere gave a bizarre touch to the usually bright little coastal resort.

The service was a memorable one, conducted by the Reverend T. Horne, who, I was given to understand, was the chaplain of the Showman's Guild, a very impressive white-bearded cleric in a white cassock worn over his black robes. He said, 'The heart of showland mourns its dead chief and leader, George Sanger . . .'

I decided to forgo the memorial supper which was to be held at one of Sanger's establishments, feeling that among hundreds of friends and relatives my absence would not even be noticed. I walked back to the station, the rain having at last relented a little, and noticed the tokens of respect everywhere with curtains drawn, flags at half mast and cab drivers' whips adorned with bows of black crêpe. I decided that if I got back to Park Farm long before the Austins, Jackson and the others, I would be able to converse with Holmes concerning Sanger's death, should his health make this possible.

There was only an elderly caretaker to greet me at Park Farm and I was about to make for the staircase in order to visit Holmes's bed of sickness when, to my amazement, my friend appeared from the drawing-room entrance, looking as fit as I have seen him. I gasped, 'Holmes, I am delighted to see you looking so much better than you did this morning. I was quite worried for you, my dear fellow.'

Holmes smiled enigmatically and said, 'My dear Watson, I was never anything but fighting fit. I anticipated a chance to have the house practically to myself by effecting a severe chill. A harmless deception but I think a quite convincing one.'

I was furious. Holmes, could you not have taken me into your confidence?' Of course it was not the first time that Holmes had practised deception upon me. I had never quite recovered from my fury when discovering that he had been camped out on Dartmoor only a mile or two from Baskerville Hall and had put me through the charade of sending reports to him at Baker Street. Neither had I forgotten the occasion when with deceipt aided by theatrics he had convinced me that was lying, expiring upon his deathbed. But I did not mention these episodes or others like them, simply enquiring, 'I suppose you used some irritant to produce the coughing and sneezing?'

He laughed, 'A little cayenne pepper goes a long way. I managed to acquire some as we left the dinner table.'

Of course my next thought was to ask if he had discovered anything of interest or advantageous. But he shook his head, saying, 'Watson, it is that which I have not found that is singular.'

He explained further. 'As soon as you were all away to the funeral I waited for the old groom who was acting as caretaker to go upon an errand to the far end of the farm. I watched him from my bedroom window, then when it was safe to do so I tackled Sanger's desk in the parlour. I was looking for the famous fifty pounds which had allegedly been stolen by Cooper; do you remember the contents of the suicide note?'

I said, 'I thought that the fifty pounds were supposed to be behind his dressing mirror. Surely it was some sort of paper connected with the lost horses that was supposed to be in his desk?'

Holmes nodded. 'Quite right, but I decided to look in the desk first before the aged retainer returned. I found no papers of the kind which I was looking for. Then hearing the footfalls of the old man as he returned I closed and relocked the desk.'

I asked, 'You had its key?'

He said, 'Why no, Watson, but I was able to open it with one of the thin blades of my penknife and secure it again the same way.'

I was a little puzzled by this uneventful episode being held up by Holmes as some sort of progress. 'You looked for the paper but did not find it. Is that all?'

He laughed. 'Why no, but elimination is useful, Watson. I hastily and silently went up the stairs and coughed and sneezed in my bedroom until I felt sure that the coast was clear. Then when he went out again I ventured forth and took a look in Sanger's bedroom.'

I ventured to enquire, 'Opening the lock with your penknife of course?' with just a hint of irony.

But Holmes said, 'No, I used a piece of wire which I bent to the correct shape by trial and error; a system which I have often used before, if you remember?'

Holmes's account of his inspection of George Sanger's bedroom was interesting and I did not interrupt him until he had clearly come to the end of his narration.

'It was an imposing room with a huge four-poster bed near the window. Just inside there was another bed, small and rather like the camp cots used by the army when under canvas. This was doubtless used by Cooper and Jackson in their turn, when Sanger's health needed watching in the night. But, to more important matters, there was indeed a wash-stand with a mirror at one side of the room and a desk at the other side. A search behind the mirror revealed nothing, but the desk, although it seemed to hold nothing of importance on first examination (by the way I needed no implement to open it as the lock was as primitive as to require only a sharp blow from the heel of my hand on the desk top to spring it) eventually yielded something quite interesting, Watson. It was a receipt book with only one printed receipt form torn from it. I therefore took a pencil to the remaining top sheet to reveal the impression of what had been written on the missing sheet; fortunately with a hard pencil. It said: "Received from Mr Foley, Twelve Hundred Pounds in full payment for twelve Royal Creams. (Signed) G. Sanger." Naturally, I tore off the sheet that I had doctored and I feel sure that Kane will not be interested enough to notice any difference. Oh, by the way, there were some splendid portraits upon the walls of the chamber, including a splendid oil of Sanger's wife Ellen Chapman with her beasts . . .'

Holmes infuriated me as he gave an inventory of the contents of Sanger's bedroom, knowing that most of this could be of no interest to me. But eventually he relented and showed me the sheet from the receipt book. I enquired, 'Is it in Sanger's hand?'

He glared at me as he said, 'The signature is, but the rest is printed by someone else of course.'

I was surprised. 'Why "of course"?'

Holmes said, 'We observed Sanger over quite a period of time, Watson. Did you ever see him write more than his name, and how often did you see him dictate notes to others to write for him?'

I asked, 'You mean he was illiterate? My dear Holmes, the man was the author of the book, *Seventy Years a Showman!*'

He chuckled. 'Also dictated to another. Probably the note was printed out in pencil by this Mr Foley who bought the Royal Creams, which of course refers to horses of a cream colour; "Royal" because they were related to the pair of cream ponies presented by Sanger to the late Queen

Victoria. The receipt by the way is dated February 17th, 1911, so I feel sure that these were the horses which Sanger was understood to infer that Cooper had some part in stealing. If we can also find the fifty pounds we will at least have cleared the poor fellow's name in part.'

That night, with the return of the Austins and a number of guests from the world of circus, further converse between Holmes and I concerning Cooper was postponed. At dinner all the talk was of George Sanger, his humble beginnings, his great enterprise and those minor deceptions which endeared him to the public rather than angering them, when sometimes one of these was revealed by the press. The 'White elephant', the 'Wolves that terrified London' and how he beat the Yankees Barnum and Cody at their own game. Sir Robert Fossett (a knight of the circus, of course) rose to propose a toast to Gentleman George, saying, 'He may not have been a real lord but, by golly, he was a real gentleman!'

We were both down early for breakfast the following morning and Holmes took advantage of our solitary state to give me another piece of information concerning the investigations he had carried out in Sanger's room. 'Watson, I quite forgot to show you this.' He held up a single key with a luggage label attached to it with a small loop of string. 'Look at the word written upon the label, Watson.'

I made out the word 'Vardo', which I confess at that time meant nothing to me. I asked, 'Where did you get this?'

He replied, 'It was in Sanger's desk in his bedroom. All night I have puzzled where I have heard that word before, and at last, about an hour ago, it came to me. It took four pipes of Scottish mixture to recall it to mind. Have you read *Lavengro*?'

I said, 'Yes, it's by George Borrow, is it not, a novel about gypsy folk?'

Holmes nodded, 'Exactly, and in that book there is a glossary of Romany words. Among them is the word "Vardo" which means a wagon, or what we would today call a caravan. This is the key to Sanger's living wagon, which I'll wager has been quite overlooked by Kane and Colman. Come, let us take a quick look inside that wagon, for the others will breakfast as soon as they are down, and the police may not return for an hour or more, if at all today.'

Sherlock Holmes strode up to the caravan and briskly opened the lock with the key without any sort of furtive behaviour. We entered the pleasantly appointed interior of the vehicle and marvelled at its compactness. There were china cabinets with cunningly devised arrangements to prevent the proudly displayed plate and ornaments from falling during the movement of the caravan. The centre table folded and lay flat against a wall when not in use, but the bed was a solid shelf, rather like a ship's bunk. There was a safe, doubtless designed to take the showman's night's takings and a dressing-table bolted to the wall opposite to the bed. Above it, part of its design, was a large oval mirror in a wooden frame. Holmes made straight for it and with the right blade on his many-purpose penknife he swiftly loosened the four screws which held the frame in place. Then he lifted down the mirror, from behind which fell a fat envelope. Its flap was merely tucked in rather than stuck down so it was easy to find what was inside. This proved to be ten folded five-pound notes. He cried, 'Just what I had hoped to find, Watson, the missing fifty pounds, behind the mirror of the washstand, but not the one we expected. So with this and an indication of the bill of sale for the horses we have borne out Cooper's claims, in his suicide note. He had suffered badly from Sanger's sudden change of feelings for him. Come, we will replace everything just as we found it; but Watson we do have the knowledge.'

He was as good as his word, replacing the screws as I held the mirror in place, with the envelope behind it. Then he gestured towards the safe. He looked at me with mischief in his eyes, 'Shall we dare risk opening it, Watson?'

I gasped at the daring of his suggestion. 'Holmes, isn't that taking things a bit far; and in any case how would you go about opening a combination safe when you do not have any idea of the numbers involved?'

Holmes grinned like a small boy and said, 'My dear Watson, I number many unsavoury characters among my circle of acquaintances. Among these is one Charlie Perkins who until his enforced retirement made a good living from opening such devices without recourse to force of any kind. He showed me how to do it, but I will need to borrow from you a stethoscope. You must have one with you, for I never knew a medical man who would go far without one.'

Of course I had a small medical bag with me and I went back to the house to fetch the instrument which Holmes needed. The family were still at breakfast and there was as yet no sign of the police. I crept up to my bedroom and having found the instrument I wedged it into my hat, which I held with its open side to my body.

To watch Holmes open that safe was an education to be sure! He wore the earpieces just as I would have done, but instead of applying the listening portion to a bare chest he held it against the front of the safe. Then with his free hand he slowly turned the numbered dial, announcing one of the numbers for me to write down each time he heard that click which would have been inaudible without the stethoscope. Without much difficulty he then turned the dial again to the numbers he had found and soon the click of the lock anticipated the opening of the safe.

There were a number of items inside to interest us. These included a locket which imprisoned a switch of auburn hair, a notebook covered in Russia leather, a few small framed pictures, and what was clearly a legal document. Holmes looked at each in turn but replaced all save the notebook and the document. He sat upon Sanger's bed and looked swiftly through the notebook. He studied some of its pages before passing it to me and making the enquiry, 'What do you make of this, Watson?'

The pages were filled not with writing as one might have expected but rather with extremely crude thumbnail sketches of people, animals and circus equipment. Near the beginning, for instance, was a page bearing a child-like scrawl which could have been taken to depict several dogs leaping out of a cage with its door open and making for a white horse. Further on there was another sheet with what could have been interpreted as a caricature of a man painting an elephant. There were many, many such drawings. Much further on there were a series of drawings depicting a man with a match and what appeared to be a blazing tent, a lion lying dead beside a piece of meat which had a skull drawn upon it and an acrobat falling from a trapeze. There were also crude sketches of elephants seemingly on the rampage and lions loose among caravans. Finally there were a number of blank pages.

I handed the volume back to my friend and said, 'I make of it that it is a child's sketch book, a child of quite tender years at that. Possibly drawn by the son or daughter of one of Sanger's performers or staff, for they all seem to depict scenes on a circus field.'

Holmes was not dismissive, 'This was my own first feeling, Watson, but however beloved a child might be I find it hard to believe that anyone would keep its drawings in a safe. I could be wrong and you could well be right, but I ask you to take another look at the images. They are child-like in their execution, I will grant you, yet there is immense detail in them. I suspect that they have been drawn by an adult of very limited artistic ability and I believe the whole thing to be a diary of events. I would ask you also to consider; there is a crude yet persistent image which occurs again and again, seemingly of a man in a frock coat and top hat with a circlet of beard upon the face. This image would appear to me to represent Sanger himself.'

I glanced again through the book and had to agree that such an interpretation could be made. I asked, 'Who, then, do you think the primitive artist might have been?'

Holmes's reply quite startled me. 'I have, as you know, reasons to believe that he was illiterate, capable of little more than scrawling his name. What better method for such a man to keep some sort of record of events than to draw them where he could not write?'

I gasped, 'A sort of almanac or diary then?'

He nodded. 'Yes, though undated for obvious reasons and dropped and picked up again from time to time. It depicts some events which are well documented. For example there were "The wolves that terrified London". Sanger has depicted himself as releasing them. Although he may not have actually done that himself we know that he caused it to happen. The same can be said of the cartoon of Sanger painting an elephant. He told us once of how much this deception to produce a "Sacred White Pachyderm" so amused the late King Edward when he was Prince of Wales! Moving on through the pages we leave the record of historic deceptions to find drawings of events which we were ourselves involved with. The poisoned lion, the trapeze accident, the aborted firing of the tent and so on.'

I gave the book another glance, then said, 'How about the drawing which appears to represent stampeding elephants, and another which shows lions escaping?'

Holmes chuckled, 'Old Sanger had those escapades planned, but thought better of them once we had discovered, as we did, that he had caused those other incidents himself. But he knew that there was a limit to my patience and that any further self-inflicted wounds would have been the cause of the end of my silence.'

Often since the incidents referred to I had wondered at how Holmes had so calmly accepted Sanger's escapades and the fact that he had really been taken advantage of for purposes of publicity. As so often happened he appeared to read my mind, saying, 'Oh come, Watson, one had to admire the bravado of the man. To be able to say that I had failed to solve his mysteries was the icing on his cake of notoriety.'

I said, 'But Holmes, however you admire the man's nerve surely you have to agree that some of his escapades were dangerous enough to be considered the work of a near lunatic?'

Sherlock Holmes paused, thoughtfully, before he replied, 'You might consider it to be so, but of course Sanger was not mad in the accepted sense, although he was very strange. The events which led up to the bizarre affair of his passing must point to Sanger having been paranoid, as Sigmund Freud would have had it. His changes of mood and of friendships point to what the unscientific would refer to as a persecution complex. Just consider also the matters of the bill of sale for the horses which he claimed to have been deprived of through theft, and of course the fifty pounds about which he constantly tortured poor Cooper.'

At first so fantastic, Holmes's words seemed after much deliberation to be believable. Though if accurate I considered that Holmes was being rather kind regarding Sanger's sanity. As he replaced the book in the safe he took up the legal document and unfurled it very carefully, having to release a ribbon which was tied in a bow around it. He said, 'This is Sanger's will, or a copy of it, because the original is in the offices of his solicitors.' He swiftly scanned the document. Had I not known him so well and for so long I would not have believed that he could have read it rather than merely perused it. But I had and I did! He handed the document to me to read, and it took me somewhat longer to make good sense of it.

THIS IS THE LAST WILL AND TESTAMENT of myself, GEORGE SANGER of Park Farm, Finchley, retired circus owner. I bequeath to my daughter HARRIET REEVE a large silver cup presented to me by the Prince and Princess of Wales, a silver jug presented to me by shareholders in Sanger Ltd, a silver punch bowl, two large candelabra, an illuminated address presented to me by the Showman's Guild on January 24th, 1906, two oil portraits of myself and my late wife, a gold medal presented to me at Boulogne March 1st, 1883, a large presentation locket with initials E.S. in pearls and diamonds. A scarf-pin in turquoise presented to me by the late Queen Victoria. A large silver cup presented by shareholders on my 70th birthday. A silver cigar box presented to me by the late Queen Victoria, a silver cup, three silver soup tureens and a silver tea and coffee service, two bronze cavaliers, two gilt busts of myself and my wife, a large portrait of myself painted in 1898.

To my Grand-daughters, ELEANOR, ERONIA, SARAH and LILLIAN, each one of the nickel horses on stands.

To my nephew GEORGE SANGER a ramshead presented to me by the Duke and Duchess of Fife, a large shield of silver, a silver cup and a portrait of Andrew Ducrow.

To my Grand-daughter ELLEN, the wife of Harry Austin, a bronze clock, an equestrian figure, a photograph of myself, all my furniture, linen, china, glass, prints, musical instruments, books, stores and provisions and all else which shall be at Park Farm upon my death save where otherwise bequested.

To my Grandson VICTOR, my gold watch and chain and a single-stone diamond ring.

To my Grand-daughter GEORGINA, an oil painting of her mother.

To HARRY AUSTIN, my carbuncle pin with star and diamond centre and a single-stone diamond ring.

To my Nephew GEORGE, my gold horse and diamond scarf pin.

I bequeath the following pecuniary legacies:

My Daughter HARRIET, fifteen thousand pounds.

My Grand-daughter ELLEN, five thousand pounds.

My Grand-daughter GEORGINA, two thousand pounds.

My Godson ARTHUR, two hundred pounds.

My Niece AMELIA, two hundred pounds.

My Niece CAROLINE, two hundred pounds.

My Niece MARY, one hundred pounds.

My Niece ANNE, one hundred pounds.

My Nephew GEORGE, one thousand pounds.

To THOMAS COOPER the elder of Park Farm, fifty pounds.

To THOMAS COOPER the younger, fifty pounds.

To HERBERT COOPER, fifty pounds.

To LEONARD COOPER, five pounds.

To JAMES CROCKET, fifty pounds.

To JULIA SANGER, fifteen hundred pounds.

My trustees shall, as soon as conveniently possible after my death, sell, call in or otherwise convert into money such parts of my premises as shall not consist of ready money and shall out of such sales pay my funeral expenses and debts and legacies. They shall hold the residue of said monies in trust for my daughter HARRIET for her sole use and benefit.

There followed Sanger's signature, such as it was, and those of witnesses. The reader will appreciate that I have given here a version of the will dragged up from my memory of quickly reading it, aided by more brief press coverage published much later when the will was read. What I have published here may well be flawed through inaccuracy.

Holmes studied it to about the same degree as I did before asking me, 'Well, Watson, what is there here that is of particular significance?'

I replied, 'Well, he has a great many nieces, and they, along with his grand-daughters, have benefited, particularly Ellen Austin. But his daughter Harriet has got the lion's share, which I suppose seems natural.'

Sherlock Holmes carefully tied the ribbon bow, to imitate exactly the appearance that it had before presented and placed the document back inside the safe. Then he said, 'I am surprised that you have not mentioned one or two points that interest me considerably. For instance, he has left fifty pounds to the late Herbert Cooper and there is no mention whatever of Jackson which means that he has come upon the scene quite recently, the will being dated barely two years ago. Certainly Jackson had become trusted and appreciated to the extent of being promoted to companion and valet in a very short time. Doubtless had Sanger lived longer he would have added to the will or altered it again.'

I jumped in quickly. 'Again?'

He nodded, there is an addition, written in by a practised hand though not the same one that drafted the original document. It appears after a series of minor bequests, some of them as low as fifty pounds, to one Julia Sanger and is for fifteen hundred pounds!'

I suppose that Sherlock Holmes and I had spent enough time with George Sanger those good few years earlier to have heard most of his relatives, friends and even mere acquaintances spoken of; yet I could not recall a Julia Sanger.

It was consoling to some extent to think that the store-house of memory that was the brain of Sherlock Holmes could not recall this name any more than could my own grey matter. We closed everything and left it as we had found it, locked the wagon and repaired to the house. Inside we found that most of the relatives mentioned in the will were present, along with their husbands and wives. We were anxious to meet the chief benefactor, Harriet, though that we knew of that fact we could not of course divulge. She proved to be a woman in middle age, of very strong personality and with something of George's strength of character in her face. She had his high cheek bones and deep sunk eyes. Whilst she also used rouge I doubt if her dark tresses were touched up with gyp. She said, 'Mr Holmes, Dr Watson, I am delighted that you are present. Although of course my father's will has yet to be read he always gave me to understand that I would inherit the bulk of his estate.'

I was relieved to think that she at least had some idea of

that which we had subversively learned. She continued, 'Now I have quite a good idea of the monies and properties involved; yet I was always puzzled at his references to some secret cache of treasure, but exactly the form it took he would not tell me. However, I was supposed to come here this very weekend to be shown this treasure. Alas, I have come to his funeral instead. Although my father was in his right mind he was a little strange in some ways as you may have realized. I have no way now of knowing to what he referred; but your visit may be a godsend. You are the most talented detective in Europe, this I know. You came here to be of service, even if posthumously to my father; you cannot help him now, but you could be of immeasurable service to me. In inheriting all that is here I might never find that which is hidden. The property will doubtless be sold eventually, and whoever buys it might stumble upon it years from now! Will you help me, sir?'

I got the impression that my friend agreed to help her as much to satisfy his own curiosity as through any wish to help this woman, who was not a charismatic personality. He said, 'I will do what I can for you, dear lady, but you will need to search your mind for any additional scrap of information that you can give me. Are you sure that he said no more than treasure in reference to this cache?'

She wrinkled her brow and said, 'Well, he did mutter some words which sounded somewhat Germanic. Kron something or other. Nothing more that I can remember.'

Intrigued, I was delighted when Holmes agreed to put his mind to Harriet Reeve's (for that was her married name) problem. He said to me, 'I could hardly tell her that Sanger had mentioned no such treasure trove in his will, for I am not supposed to have seen it. But I am intrigued by the promise of treasure trove, perhaps in the form of a cache of jewels, and the hint of a Germanic Kron.'

We walked in the meadow with Holmes deep in thought, his head almost on his chest. Suddenly my friend raised his head and said, 'Upon my word, is it possible? Unlikely, yet it all seems to fit. The German word Kron refers to a crown, and we are looking for jewels perhaps. So maybe Sanger said, Kronjuwelen? The Austro-Hungarian crown jewels were stolen some fifteen years ago and never retrieved. When we travelled with Sanger for a while he had a parade carriage in the form of a glass case on wheels in which he exhibited what purported to be accurate copies of the crown jewels of the British Empire. Remember, Watson, I once remarked that the case was not even locked! Whilst I never examined those crown jewels I feel sure that no one else did. There was never even any attempt to steal what were thought to be next-to-worthless copies. Remember how ruthless Sanger was when it came to his show business. Could it be possible that he received the Austrian crown jewels buying them from some desperate thief at a bargain price . . . so much of a bargain as to be almost as reasonable as having those copies made?'

I was aghast at such a thought and tried to be a devil's advocate. 'Would the public or authorities have recognized them for what they were?'

He said, 'I doubt it, trailing a float depicting Britannia and the lion I'll wager the differences would not occur to anyone. After all, Watson, one set of crown jewels is very like another.'

Holmes was no nearer to finding what had happened to those fake jewels, but at least he felt that he knew just what he was looking for. He said, 'Sanger held a sale of animals and properties soon after his retirement. We must search the lists of items auctioned for some sort of clue. He was too shrewd to have sold the Austrian crown jewels as fakes, surely, but stranger things have happened, Watson, especially where there is a hint of illegality.'

Harry Austin it was who produced the list of sale transactions for the auction. It was lengthy, covering many closely handwritten foolscap sheets. There were elephants at one hundred and fifty pounds each, a circus tent at two thousand pounds, a group of forest-bred lions, a bargain at two hundred pounds for all five. There were wagons and cages, apes, horses, ponies, llamas, camels, bandcarts, musical instruments, velvet drapes, ring fences, plank seating, folding chairs, pay boxes, living wagons, flying trapeze equipment, elephant tubs, lion pedestals, a leopard, two tigers, three Jacob four-horned sheep, four Himalayan bears and two of the polar variety, costumes for clowns, equestrians and acrobats, donkeys, mules and the Buffalo Bill stage coach.

So the list went seemingly endlessly on; each item given the price realized and by whom paid. Many were the signatures, ranging from neat copperplate to indifferent scrawls, even the odd cross.

Suddenly I spotted something which I felt more than relevant to our search; 'Lot 381. Parade wagon, finished in gold leaf, four-wheeled with glass sides, made to accommodate Sanger's imitation crown jewels. £100. Sir Robert Fossett.'

We enquired of Harry Austin regarding the whereabouts of Sir Robert Fossett, expecting perhaps to be directed to some stately home. However, it transpired that 'Sir' Robert was a 'Knight of the circus' rather as Sanger had been a 'Lord of the sawdust ring'. His circus, for he had been one of Sanger's rivals, was to be found in Guildford in Surrey, where it was spending the last of a three-day stand.

Holmes confided this discovery to Harriet Reeve, who provided us with a brougham complete with horse and driver. We left almost at once, but it was late afternoon before we reached the long meadow which accommodated Sir Robert Fossett's International Circus. The big tent, which was a shade smaller than that which we remembered from our days on the tober with Sanger, was none the less extremely smart with its dark blue stripes on a yellow ground. Unlike Sanger's menagerie quadrant there was another, lesser version of the big tent, erected alongside it and accommodating the horses, lions and elephants. There were less-wild animals to be seen than with Sanger, but rather more horses; handsome creatures too, mostly in a uniform skewbald. We had learned enough not to ask to see Sir Robert at that time, because the early evening performance was about to commence and the time was not right. Instead we purchased two ringside seats and watched what was a very enjoyable performance, all but matching the mighty Sanger enterprise. The main difference, however, seemed to be in that despite its international banner it appeared to be very much a family affair with almost every red-haired, blue-eyed performer turning out later to be a Fossett. There were Fossetts who rode the broad-backed skewbalds, Fossetts who flew through the air with the greatest of ease, Fossetts who directed the elephants and showed the lions, and Funny Harry the clown who was very funny indeed and also was a Mr Tom Fossett when out of the ring.

As for Sir Robert, well he was not only the owner of this thriving enterprise but also its star attraction as 'Britain's

Champion Jockey Rider'. In racing silks and cap he leapt upon the back of a fast circling horse and removed and held aloft its saddle as he stood one-footed upon its back. He skipped upon its back, using his riding switch as a skipping rope, and leapt up onto it with baskets strapped onto his feet. He wore medals and a fiercely waxed moustache; he was an imposing sight.

As 'God Save the King' was played, all but on key by the brass band stationed over the ring entrance we looked around for someone who could direct us to the great man's presence. As the public trickled out of the tent Funny Harry stood on the ring fence, waving to them in a delight-fully jovial fashion. I dared to address this merry man in his motley and pointed hat. 'Excuse me, sir, is there any chance that we might see Sir Robert? My friend is Sherlock Holmes, the detective.'

'Ooh!' The funny fellow pretended to have the wind taken out of his sails. He said, 'What has Uncle Bob done now, snaffled a paloney?' We laughed dutifully and fol-lowed him as he beckoned us to follow him through the ring entrance. 'Guv'nor, there's a "defective" to see you, says his name is Sheerluck Jones!'

Robert Fossett shook hands with us gravely, saying, 'Take no notice of Funny Harry. What can I do for you, gentle-men? I warn you I have another performance to supervise shortly. Meanwhile you are welcome to a cup of tea in the wagon.'

Sir Robert's living wagon proved to be an even larger one than Sanger's, though I ventured to think that this might not have been so had Sanger still been on the road. Who knows, perhaps he might even have bought himself a mo-tor caravan. But I could see that Fossett's still travelled entirely by horse power, and I estimated that at least a hundred animals would be needed to move the circus.

We gratefully swallowed thick sweet tea out of the delicate china cups so beloved of showmen. Fossetts came and Fossetts went, all with blue eyes and red hair and every one of them brimming over with good nature and energy. After a little genial chatter, Holmes brought the subject round to Sanger. Sir Robert said, 'Lord George was a great man. I went to his funeral of course, but I had to come straight back, I'd missed one performance as it was. Yes, he was a great man, but just a trifle strange. What is it you want to know about him?'

Holmes mentioned the glass carriage which Fossett had purchased in the sale of a few years back. He said, 'Oh, the old glass cart. I keep two pythons in it, in my zoo tent. It is ideal for snakes, as I have no crown jewels to exhibit.'

I asked, 'You did not then purchase those along with the vehicle?'

He said, 'Bless you no, I was not interested in them and anyway they did not seem to be on offer. But there was another omhy there, a German, who asked about them. I've heard that, since then, he has rented old Sanger's practice barn to experiment with some kind of a model flying machine. Clock, or Cloak or something, his name was.'

Holmes suggested, 'Klauk?'

Fossett nodded, 'That's him!'

I gasped, though quietly, and I could tell that Holmes was also taken aback. He said, 'Sir Robert, you have not only entertained us well but have given us a very valuable piece of information. We will take no more of your valuable time and will bid you farewell and good tenting.' Fossett accompanied us to our equipage, pausing only to terrify some urchins who were attempting to crawl under the canvas of the menagerie tent.

We returned to Park Farm at quite a spanking pace, but it was still quite late when we got there. During most of the journey we had of course quietly discussed the possibilities presented by the information we had received concerning Herr Klauk. Holmes had mused, 'We have to decide if we can believe in a situation of coincidence, Watson. Could it possibly be coincidental that a German professor is in residence at Park Farm, where we now begin to suspect that the Austrian crown jewels are concealed?'

I had to opine that I thought a coincidence unlikely. I ventured, 'Can we perhaps learn something about Klauk from our own contacts, Holmes?'

My friend took my point at once. 'Lestrade might be able to help us, for although retired I feel sure that he still has a finger on the pulse of things. Tomorrow we might visit him at Hampstead, but tonight the game is afoot!'

It was one of the clock before we ventured forth into the grounds of Park Farm to attempt some kind of search for the possibility of finding the Austro-Hungarian crown jewels. Holmes had constructed a wire implement with which I assumed that he intended to search the barn occupied by Klauk for his aerial experiments. We entered the building fairly easily through that means but our search by lantern light proved fruitless. We inspected every open cupboard and alcove first, then picked the locks of other places of possible concealment without finding more than those items which one might expect an engineer and model-maker to possess. We even investigated the possibilities of the floor, but could find no sign of replaced or repaired floorboards. In desperation we even searched the basket that was attached to the model airship which was docked with blocks and supports at one end of the building, but without success.

Taking advantage of the dark and the solitude we searched as much of the rest of the farm outbuildings as we could, short of disturbing man or beast. But in the end we had to return to our beds without having discovered any sort of clue that would aid our investigations.

Harriet Reeve was happy to give us the use of her carriage again on the following day when we made the short journey to Hampstead, making a detour, however, that I might, at Holmes's suggestion, collect my service revolver from my home. This gave me the opportunity to also obtain some fresh linen.

George Lestrade was glad to see us and had changed but little since last we had met. He dispensed tea and biscuits in his sitting-room as he and Holmes reminisced about old times, old cases and old triumphs. But eventually Holmes managed to bring the conversation round to that which we wanted to speak of. 'My dear Lestrade, I feel sure that you recollect the theft of the Austrian crown jewels?'

Lestrade nodded. 'It happened about fifteen years ago; there was a hue and cry for them among all the police forces in Europe, but they were never found. There is still a very substantial reward offered in Austria for them. But whoever had them would have to get them there secretly, for anywhere else he would be arrested, reward or no!'

Holmes asked, 'There is no international agreement, then, concerning this matter?'

Lestrade grinned. 'With the strong feelings between France and Germany and war averted only recently, co-operation is at its lowest ebb.'

There was a pause, then Holmes asked, 'What do you know concerning one Herr Klauk?'

Lestrade bristled. 'German inventor, strong nationalist, the secret service people have their eyes on his activities.' His eyes opened wide when Holmes told him of the Sanger affair, the Cooper tragedy, but most especially the presence of Klauk in Sanger's barn. He asked, 'Who is on the Sanger case?'

Holmes told him. 'Chief Inspector Kane and Detective Sergeant Colman.'

Lestrade said little but shook his head sadly. He said, 'Not much use asking them to help. I would go in on your own if the opportunity presents itself. But go easy, Kane is a tartar and a stickler for procedure.'

That evening our attention was taken from the matter of Klauk and his possible involvement with the Austrian crown jewels. We were making a quiet search of the grounds at the farm when we came upon a quiet area which had previously escaped our notice. There were a number of small graves marked by miniature headstones and crosses. At first I took it to be a children's cemetery and was thinking how very sad it was when Holmes pointed to one of the headstones: 'Gussie. A Goose with Character'.

I gasped, 'A goose, Holmes? Why, when a goose dies it usually does so that people might eat it!'

Holmes nodded, 'But we are in the world of the circus, where a goose is as good as his master, if he is a performer. Look here too . . .' He pointed with his cane at another inscription: 'Charlie. 1882–1896. A very small dog, but a very great artiste.' I have to tell the reader that it was sheer chance that it was I who made the 'discovery'! 'Great heavens, Holmes.' It was my turn to point with a cane. 'Look at this!' My cane tip hovered over the inscription: 'Julia Sanger (1901–1910) A monkey who was the much-loved companion of Lord George Sanger. Sleep peacefully, dear little friend.'

Sherlock Holmes chuckled as he said, 'Well done, Watson. You have spotted that which clears the mystery of that added note in Sanger's will. The monkey was left fifteen hundred pounds, but died just a few months before she could take advantage of this windfall!'

I said, 'Surely, this must point to Sanger having been quite out of his mind?'

But my friend shook his head. 'I had a maiden aunt who willed a thousand pounds to her pet pomeranian. She left this world with all her senses intact. It is not uncommon for an elderly person to will money to a treasured pet, to ensure that the animal is cared for.'

On our way back to the house we passed Klauk who was transporting a number of cylinders upon a wheelbarrow. He nodded brightly to us and we returned his salutation in a manner which ensured that he might not be alerted to any of our suspicions. When he had transported the cylinders into the barn and we were well out of earshot I said, 'I wonder what those cylinders are for?'

But there was no puzzlement in Holmes's voice as he replied, 'Gas of some kind, to fuel his model airship. This must indicate that his experiments have reached a final stage and that he intends shortly to make his model airborne.'

We risked mentioning the matter to Harry Austin who told us, 'I do not know, understand or care about his experiments, but I do know that he has given me notice that he wishes to vacate the barn shortly and has paid me rents and charges in final settlement.'

On the following day we asked Harriet if we might invite a friend, one George Lestrade, to stay at the farm in order that he might aid our investigations. She agreed without question and sent her carriage for him. He arrived later, complete with an overnight bag, and with a broad grin on his face. 'Like old times, Mr Holmes. When I got your wire I dropped everything and here I am.'

We told Lestrade of the arrival of the gas cylinders and of the imminent departure of Klauk. His eyes narrowed, though he was less impressed with the news about Julia Sanger. However, he was genial enough concerning Holmes's suggestion that he should see the monkey's grave. As we strolled towards the little cemetery he enquired, 'What puzzles me is just why you want me here, Holmes. I'm sure you are capable of handling the situation?'

Holmes took out his pipe and tobacco, offering some to Lestrade and they both charged their pipes before Holmes replied. I preferred to smoke a cigar. Then at length Holmes said, 'Your advice is valuable, Inspector, but I admit that my main reason for my wanting your presence is that I need a witness, other than Watson, to certain events which may or may not happen. Who better than an ex-inspector of detectives, late of Scotland Yard. Aye, and who worse than the present chief inspector, Kane, whose grasp of events does not match yours, Lestrade.'

He was flattered. 'I see, well I'll be happy to bear witness to whatever happens. But be warned I can only be an honest witness, so please stay well within the law.'

We had reached the pet cemetery, and Holmes had listed his cane to indicate the Julia Sanger inscription when he gasped, 'Upon my word, the monkey's grave has been tampered with since we looked at it last evening.' He was right, the turf, although returned to its position had been clearly moved. 'Watson, fetch a spade and do it as quietly as you can.' I wandered back towards the house, being fortunate enough to come upon a spade, near a heap of turnips, which I took back to my friend.

Holmes grabbed the spade from me and with it, displaying surprising strength and agility, turned back the layer of turf to reveal the loose and recently disturbed earth below. He dug the loose earth out and found only a heap of stones beneath. He grunted, 'A hiding place for something and a good one. Had we not taken an entirely illegal glance at George Sanger's will we would never have lingered here long enough to notice the change that had taken place. Oh yes, Inspector, I will take the responsibility for my subversive behaviour.'

Holmes continued, 'Whatever he does, and I feel sure that he will soon take some action, it will be under cover of darkness. We must watch this very night to see what occurs.' Holmes drilled us so that we knew what we had to do. 'I'm sure you have a whistle, Lestrade, and I never go anywhere without one. I suggest that you observe from the house side of the barn and Watson and I will watch from the far side. If you see anything that requires action, blow your whistle and I will come. I also will blow mine if I need you on my side. But I cannot emphasize enough that we should only raise such an alarm as a last resort. We do not wish to alert our quarry until it is necessary.'

That night at dinner Holmes introduced Lestrade to the company as his friend George Lever, a retired actor. He sprung this introduction onto Lestrade who winced uncomfortably, but played up well. I appreciated why Holmes had given this new character his original initials because

Lestrade had arrived carrying an overnight bag marked 'G.L.', and for all he knew Lestrade might have brought initialled towels and linen. The circus people were interested to meet a fellow performer, even if a legitimate one. Ellen Austin enquired, 'What plays have you been in, Mr Lever?'

Lestrade stuttered a little as he said, 'Oh, Shakespeare's *Much Ado About Nothing*, for instance.' When asked which part he had played, he said, 'Polonius, but of course I'm retired now!'

Someone was heard to murmur, 'Not surprised, Polonius is in *Hamlet!*'

Half an hour later Holmes and I were hidden by some bushes on the far side of Sanger's barn. Lestrade had secreted himself in a shed on the near side which had a handy window for him to observe from out through its dark interior. For the better part of an hour there was nothing to observe. Then suddenly Holmes pinched my arm and said, 'Look, Watson, look at the roof!' Sure enough a portion of the roof had opened. Then very calmly, Holmes said, 'As I suspected he is about to send the crown jewels of Austro-Hungary up into the sky.'

Sure enough, almost at once, there arose the silver, cigar shape of the little airship. Its gases lifted it, and a small engine propelled it once it had reached a considerable height. Klauk emerged from the barn with triumph in his face. But Holmes turned to me and said, 'Quick, Watson. Stop the airship!'

I gasped, 'How can I do that?'

He breathed heavily, 'With your service revolver, of course.'

I fired twice before I observed any result. Then to my relief the ship's engine ceased and the sphere itself burst suddenly into flames. Within seconds it was a skeleton afire, and dropped like a descending meteorite. Holmes blew his whistle which quickly brought Lestrade to our side and we all three made for the blazing metal frame. As it hit the ground, sending up a shower of sparks, we neared it with care. But Sherlock Holmes managed to pull the basket clear with the crook of his cane before it was too seriously ablaze. As I beat out the flames on the basket, Holmes and Lestrade gave chase to the fast retreating Klauk. As I pulled the charred basket from the burning frame of the model airship I opened it to find that wrapped up in sacking within were the crowns, sceptre and other pieces that we had suspected might be there.

Whilst all this was happening Klauk appeared upon the scene, frantic for the safety of his airship and its cargo. 'Gott in Himmel! What have you done to mine beautiful airship?' His mixture of languages highlighted his anxiety. Jackson was sent to fetch the police, but until the arrival of Detective Sergeant Colman, George Lestrade kept a firm hand upon Klauk's arm. Neither the ex-inspector nor Holmes had any official power, but obviously they both felt that they must take action and explain the reasons for it later.

When Colman arrived to take charge, Holmes was required to do just that, in order that the sergeant would know just what reason he had for detaining Klauk. Holmes was more than ready for his narration.

'Klauk is not only a clever inventor, but a patriot for the royalist faction of his government. Some years ago he learned of the crown jewels being hidden in this country. He managed to regain them but due to the political situation in Austria could not take them back there safely.

Possibly by chance he came upon Sanger's parade with its crystal coach crown jewels display. He showed great ingenuity in substituting the Austrian jewels for the Sanger facsimiles, which were doubtless discarded. This was not difficult to effect because, as I myself discovered, Sanger never even bothered to lock the glass door of the carriage. Klauk felt secure regarding the jewels whilst Sanger was on the road with them but when Sanger retired he decided to rent the barn so that he could keep an eye on developments. He was of course genuinely concerned with the invention of airships and decided to use his experiments with scale models as both a cover for his presence and a fruitful use for his time.

'Then Sanger rather took the wind out of his sails by holding a sale of his animals and effects, including his vehicles. Fortunately for him, Fossett, who bought the carriage, was not interested in what he believed to be cheap imitation crown jewels. To his relief Sanger stowed them in, I imagine, a potting shed or some such storage place which I never actually discovered. With Sanger dead, of course, the alarm bells must have started to ring in his mind. When Watson and I, as well as the police, started poking around the farm he evidently decided to change the place of concealment of the jewels. We had inspected the animal cemetery, and quite by chance we again were there to find that the monkey's grave had been disturbed since our first look at it. Klauk had buried the jewels there overnight whilst making his final preparations to fly the jewels across the Channel in the basket beneath his model airship! I anticipated this when I found the turf and earth disturbed and when I saw him wheeling the gas cylinders towards the barn. Recent changes in

Austrian politics had made this politic, but he would still have found it impossible to remove the items from Britain by any official route. Far too many questions would have been asked, and he was engaged in any case in espionage.) I felt sure that developments were such, and the situation had become hot enough, for Klauk to act this very night.'

Colman was still a little uncomfortable, asking, 'I could charge Herr Klauk with theft of Sanger's jewels, if such they had been, but as they are not, what, Mr Holmes, do you suggest?'

Holmes smiled grimly. 'Endangering the safety of the realm, Sergeant! A larger version of that airship could be a menace in time of war.'

Alas, Holmes's words were prophetic, as we were to discover within less than half a decade.

So ended our involvement with the affairs of Lord George Sanger. In investigating them Sherlock Holmes had gone some way towards clearing the name of Herbert Cooper. Alas, the words 'Unlawful Killing' would appear in the inquest verdict, but the word 'Murder' was not involved. Klauk proved to be involved in a number of episodes which in time of war would have carried a death sentence. Doubtless the Austrians would also be grateful to Holmes for the return of their crown jewels without involving a dubious third party.

Holmes requested that I should not publish an account of the Sanger episode until a considerable time had elapsed following the showman's death.

'After all, Watson, those who read your narrative might consider some of his actions to be those of a man deranged; for they did not know him as well as we did.'

I considered, 'Would you perhaps refer to Lord George as "The British Barnum"?'

He puffed thoughtfully at his favourite clay, then replied, 'On the contrary. I might be tempted to refer to Barnum as "The American Sanger"!'